Paro

Dreams of Passion

'A magnificent creation' – *London Magazine*

'The first full-length novel by an Indian woman that unabashedly dealt with sexual themes' – *Times of India*

'Never has a novel cut to the chase about middle class mores with such fearless and sensual prose'
– Cauvery Madhavan, author of *The Inheritance*

To AAI

ALSO BY NAMITA GOKHALE

Never Never Land
The Blind Matriarch
Jaipur Journals
Mystics and Sceptics: In Search of Himalayan Masters
Treasures of Lakshmi
Things to Leave Behind

Paro

Dreams of Passion

Namita Gokhale

HOPEROAD

HopeRoad Publishing Ltd
c/o Peepal Tree Press
17 Kings Avenue
Leeds LS6 1QS

First published in the UK by Chatto & Windus, 1984.
This edition published in the UK 2025 by HopeRoad
www.hoperoadpublishing.com

A CIP catalogue record for this book is available from
the British Library.

ISBN: 978-1-913109-39-4
e-ISBN: 978-1-913109-48-6

Supported using public funding by
ARTS COUNCIL
ENGLAND

INTRODUCTION
by
MAYA JAGGI

Namita Gokhale's relentlessly candid satire of sexual liberation and social climbing in urban, post-independence India elicited praise and outrage in equal measure when it was first published in 1984. Bristling with mischievous observations on the upper-middle-class cocktail circuits of New Delhi and Bombay (now Mumbai), *Paro: Dreams of Passion* scandalised with its unabashed frankness about women's sexual desire in and outside marriage, at a time when Bollywood struggled to show even kissing on screen. Yet perhaps most shocking was that the novel made male (and female) vanity, sexual double standards, and the preening entitlement of workplace 'Romeos', into the butt of laughter.

Conceived as a confessional diary, it charts the obsession of the narrator Priya, a 'voyeur and diarist', with Paro, a brigadier's daughter and femme fatale whom Priya loathes, envies and wishes to be. While 'most women marry the best provider they can stomach,' the grey-green-eyed, gin-swilling Paro follows her own voracious appetites, netting Priya's boss and 'dreamboat' lover, B.R, before discarding him for a trail of sexual conquests: Lenin, the 'harmless' Marxist son of a cabinet minister; Bucky Bhandpur, princely test cricketer;

Shambhu Nath Mishra, Congress Party politician; and Loukas Leoras, Greek homosexual film director. As force-of-nature Paro grasps all the alimony she can, she tells Priya, 'They wrote the rules.'

Priya, an outside onlooker from Bombay's suburban lower middle class, saw her dreams of college collapse when family savings were lavished on a less clever brother who repeatedly flunked his medical exams. After a secretarial stint at Sita Sewing Machines ('The Housewife's Friend'), when the ingénue Priya was seduced in an opulent apartment overlooking Bombay's Marine Drive, an arranged marriage to an assiduously upwardly-mobile New Delhi lawyer brings her back into Paro's orbit. At a time of encroaching Western mores, Priya vacillates between adulterous passions and abject efforts to convince herself that, 'I am an Indian woman and for me my husband is my God.' Her fear and ambivalence at following Paro's lead are implicitly rooted in the terrors of reputational damage and destitution as an abandoned woman, with the dismal prospect of surviving as a poor relation and unpaid ayah to her sister-in-law's brood.

Echoes of Daphne du Maurier's *Rebecca* (Priya's favourite novel) and Charlotte Brontë's *Jane Eyre* combine with knowing nods to Mills & Boon, gothic novels, Hindi Romances and 'filmi' melodrama. While Gokhale's sharp satirical wit has precedents in Jane Austen and Muriel Spark, a local reality beyond the privileged jet-set characters memorably intrudes – in the slum children who are said to watch their parents copulate without traumatic ill-effect, or the road-user knocked off his donkey by a Scotch-sodden driver who casually pays him off with a paltry banknote.

The plot comes to a head on the eve of the Asian Games in New Delhi in 1982. Yet it is testament to the appeal it holds for successive generations that this serio-comic début novel of lust, lucre, sex and suicide has never been out of print. Written in English (with some untranslated lines of Hindustani) when the author was twenty-six, and originally published by Chatto & Windus in London, *Paro* marked its 40th anniversary in 2024, reissued in India as a Penguin Modern Classic.

Is the enigmatic Paro a feminist paragon – as some have claimed – a manipulative minx, or a tragic scapegoat whose inner contradictions mirror those of a society in the throes of transition? As 'women's lib' lapped the globe, did the author sense the limitations of sexual freedom unaccompanied by economic independence or a shift in power? It is partly such ambiguities, and its openness to interpretation, that make Paro an enduring classic.

Maya Jaggi
London 2025

I am writing about them because I saw myself in her.

I was B.R.'s secretary at that time; all of us at the office thought he was a real dreamboat. He looked straight into our eyes – he knew all our first names – and he was a compulsive nymphomaniac. The dictionary says that a male nymphomaniac is properly described as a victim of satyriasis, but I think that he was a nymphomaniac; and I think it was related to his compulsive need to sell himself.

He was short, but he hadn't begun to go bald – and he was our boss. Ivy, Mary and I loved him madly; and all of us hated Paro. She would breeze into the office every now and then, and appraise us through narrowed green-grey eyes. Her eyes mocked us and they mocked our devotion to B.R.

B.R. had decorated the office himself. It was like the temple of Pallas Athene for us. The clear white lines of Formica, the immaculate swivel chairs, the perfectly tended potted plants, as perfectly tended as the oyster-pale nails of his personal secretary. (It was only her bouffant that was a little ruffled, that and her expression, when she emerged from the sanctum sanctorum after taking private dictation.)

B.R.'s company manufactured the famous Sita Sewing Machines, and associated household goods. The company's motto of 'The Housewife's Friend' reverberated like an echo through its offices and corridors.

In splendid Gothic lettering, it was accompanied by a gigantic colour blow-up of our consumer, The Housewife, as envisaged by B.R. and the whiz-kids from the publicity dept. The Housewife was a blowsy, voluptuous woman who bestowed come-hitherish looks on a resplendent sewing machine while her husband stood timidly searching his pockets for his hanky in the middle foreground.

I see him as he is now – and he is very different. His hair, which to my besotted eyes had as much vitality in its every black root as in his every magical gesture or action, is now plastered vainly over his balding forehead. He is prematurely grey at forty-six, and the salt-and-pepper hair on his hirsute, softly undulating chest is always exposed all the way to the bulging belly-button. The cool, calculated poise of his mannerisms seem unreal, as indeed it is, hiding as it does an almost phobic terror and insecurity. His voice, so musical then in its masculine timbre, sounds a little fruity now – he is, I must confess, a much diminished man.

And I think of Paro, as I saw her last, flushed with drink and anger. And I think of the sea at Marine Drive, the first time that he kissed me – vast, ugly and compulsive. I yielded almost immediately to the pressure of his plastic lips; but a part of me held back, observant and detachedly clinical. I stared instead at the coy moon hiding behind the white clouds, and watched the restless ocean regurgitate its teeming refuse back on to the black sullen rocks.

I remember the touch of his hands, and his suddenly gentle tongue, and the overpowering smell of his cologne, and the hardness between his legs, and the murmured words of love. My heart was pounding wildly, and I quite forgot there was a world outside.

But a narielpani-wala disturbed us, insistently holding out two obscene-looking coconuts. The evening papers were full of some mass-murderer those days, and I could glimpse a madness and hatred in his obsessive staring eyes as he insisted that we buy one.

Still B.R.'s hands continued tender, yet insistent, in their proficient ministrations to my breasts, and eternity lay before us.

For days I lay swooning in a lush romantic haze. My insides would bump against my heart every time I even thought of him. My life changed completely. I cannot really remember those days, except that every second was bathed in grace. Then, one Friday, I saw Anita, his private secretary. Her bouffant and her expression were both in a familiar state of disarray.

A month later, he was married to Paro. It took all of us at the office completely by surprise. I have never forgotten, nor forgiven, a hurt. This book, too, is a vindication.

My favourite author, when I was nineteen, was Daphne du Maurier. My favourite novel was, of course, *Rebecca*. B.R.'s flat lay like a jewel in the palm of Bombay, and in our dreams we often traipsed wraithlike through its gracious environs.

The first time I went there was on a weekend when B.R.'s father was out of town. I had never seen so much beauty before. I was spellbound by the opulence and the quietude. The azure carpeting, the dazzling white of the walls, the Ajanta fresco painted on the drawing-room wall, all held me in incredulous thrall.

I stopped to examine a convoluted sculpture in wood and metal that stood majestically in a corner. 'What's that?' I asked curiously.

'It's by Haaden,' he said proudly. 'He was heavily influenced by Henry Moore. Very phallic, you know.'

I looked up 'phallic' in my dictionary that night, and was shocked to discover what it meant, and that people could use the word so casually, or indeed so display such sculptures in their drawing-rooms.

He led me like a princess into his bedroom. Gently, he poured me some wine in a stemmed glass. It was my first taste of alcohol. It tasted heady and strange, as did everything else in the incredible new world that was unfolding bravely about me.

'Do you like classical Western compositions, love?' he asked me gravely. Mutely, I agreed that I did. He glided across to the built-in stereo system and pondered for a while over the records. 'Stravinsky,' he intoned dreamily. 'The Rites of Spring.' A strange beatification, a feeling of utter lassitude, overtook me. I forgot that my nails were as chewed and bitten as a schoolgirl's pencils, and that my sandals had gaping mouths in them. I felt beautiful. And beloved. Very gently, he stroked my hair. He undid my plait and let it lie loose about my shoulders. His soft white hands caressed my neck. His fingers were long and slim. Perfect half-moons rose mystically from each cuticle. I was mesmerised by his presence and the music. His hand slid softly down the front of my blouse and began stroking my breast. I pretended to be so lost in the music as not to have noticed. After some time the hand withdrew. One eyebrow rose quizzically over his magical eyes. 'Come with me to the balcony,' he commanded.

Marine Drive lay below us. His voice was as insistent, and as insinuating, as the rhythmic sea. It was high tide. 'Priya...' he breathed. The moonlight shone on a ghost-like jungle of cacti, crotons, bougainvillea, and all kinds of plants I did not recognise. The humid seabreeze was laden with floral nightsmells. A single pubic hair began itching beneath my blue nylon panties. The feeling spread. He led me back to the bedroom and took me there.

Later he read me some poetry which I did not understand.

B.R. had been making frequent business trips to Delhi. None of us suspected anything out of the ordinary.

Then, one afternoon, the office grapevine began buzzing with the astounding news that he was to be married in a week. Anita was put to work on the invitation list, and the typists' pool was told to dump everything else and start typing envelopes. Everyone was quite breathless with excitement, and an air of frenetic gaiety percolated through to everybody in the office. We, the staff, were all invited to bless the newly-weds at the wedding ceremony, and to the reception thereafter.

Ivy, Mary and Anita were all heartbroken. I wasn't. I listened coldly to all their excited chatter about the continuing search for the Right Gift. We, the staff, were to give them a joint present. All of us pooled together with a contribution of Rs. 25 each. I do not know what they bought because I did not go to the wedding, or to the reception either.

The day after, the girls at the office were all agog with tales of her beauty and B.R.'s obvious infatuation with her. My curiosity was aroused, and soon got the better of my pride. I wanted to see her beauty with my own eyes, and decided to attend the party the office staff was hosting for them the next evening. I took the day off, and spent the morning, and most of the afternoon, at the beautician's.

My eyebrows sometimes stand up straight at odd angles. The Chinese girl who tried to coax them into shape got a little carried away and left the right side a little off-centre, giving my face a faintly comical expression. The fashionably thin line of the eyebrows also made me look very strained. Then they bleached my upper lip; the peroxide gave me a painful and very pink rash, and it looked as if I had drunkenly gashed the lipstick a few inches above target. I even decided to get my hair permed. It was a painful decision, and cost sixty rupees, which was one-tenth of my monthly salary.

The hairdresser's assistant could, with unerring instinct, smell out my somewhat dubious social status and did his best to knot the curlers and nets into the most uncomfortable configuration possible. When I emerged from the cocoon of the dryer I had not, to my intense disappointment, turned into any butterfly. The assistant presented the mirror with a malicious flourish, and I found myself face-to-face with a stranger, and a decidedly unattractive stranger at that. My everyday face had, as I can see in retrospect, a certain robust charm, but I was certainly not looking my best the day I first met Paro.

I took a bus back, carefully protecting my hairdo on the way. On my arrival home I found my mother and brother sitting glumly at the dining table. My brother Atul, who was studying to become a doctor, had apparently flunked yet another examination. My mother had been widowed as long as I could remember, and was so like a filmi mother that I sometimes wondered whether all the scriptwriters around had used her as their particular model. Or perhaps it was the other way around, and it was in the embryonic dark of the cinema hall that she had picked up all those inflections of love and maternal solicitude. Anyway, those emotions were rarely directed at me. In actual fact I barely existed for her. Family circumstances had more or less forced me to take up a secretarial course rather than complete college; all our family savings went into making my brother a doctor. As there was no prospect of our being able to shell out any dowry for me, my mother forbode a bleak spinsterhood. 'Perhaps she will find some deaf-mute to marry her', she would mutter with gloomy relish. And yet she was full of venom at my 'fastness'; it was not in Raipur as it was in Bombay, 'and even a deaf-mute would expect his wife to be respectable.' I was, of course, the only earning member of my family.

Anyway, there they were, suspended as ever in timeless gloom, hugging their glasses of tea close to their chests. They looked a little aghast at my 'fashionable' appearance; my mother asked me querulously whether I was, after all, going to the office dinner.

They were very upset that I had not gone to the wedding reception, for the card had been duly displayed for the benefit of our neighbours, who were constantly regaled with stories, mostly apocryphal, about my boss's wealth and munificence. When I told her that I was going, she sniffed and offered me the generous loan of her Benarsi silk sari, which offer I politely declined. I had already decided to wear my red chiffon, the one I had worn the momentous night that B.R. took me home. To my dismay I found it covered with blotchy wine-stains. I got out the ironing board and tried to remove them with damp handkerchiefs. Perhaps a tear or two splashed down to help.

I borrowed my mother's gold bangles; I had to struggle with soapwater and cold cream before I could manage to get them to fit my large bony wrists. They jangled in confident affirmation of my femininity – two gold, six red glass, and then two gold again. They looked quite pretty, I thought. My new gold sandals completed the ensemble. I looked long and deep into the mirror. I knew I was not beautiful, but I felt I was special, somehow. I left hurriedly in search of a taxi. In a moment of bravado, I plucked a bright red hibiscus flower from the hedge outside the building and pinned it behind my right ear, beneath the dangling gold jhumka.

It was almost nine by the time I got there, and yet the newly-weds had not arrived. B.R.'s father, who was chairman of the company, kept repeating apologetically, 'After all, just married, you know, just married!' He wasn't in the least like a filmi father, and in fact looked closer to a filmi villain. And he was a Rai Bahadur, to boot.

His moustache was a thin grey line, trimmed from both above and below. His face wore a stern leer. 'Arrey, Priya Beti,' he said effusively, his large moist hands guiding me insistently through the room. It was obvious that he had already had too much to drink, and his hands strayed to my midriff.

Out of the corner of my eye I saw B.R. and Paro walk into the room. Rai Bahadur rushed to receive them. She was wearing a silver tissue sari, and was positively glittering with diamonds. They were strewn like dewdrops over her – chokers, pendants, rings, bangles, sequins. Tall as she was, she was balancing on the highest stiletto heels I had ever seen in my life. Even her payals were encrusted with incredibly real-looking diamonds. Her lipstick was a pale silver, and silver eyeshadow gleamed over her hard eyes. 'Hi, Daddyji,' she said throatily, planting a kiss smack on Rai Bahadur's forehead – she had to bend over slightly to reach him. Her audacity and self-confidence took my breath away. This was not how brides behaved in my world. All the brides I had ever encountered kept their sari pallavs covered, and their heads so perilously downcast as to appear anatomically endangered. But she stood proud and straight, and led the way, with B.R. and her parents trailing after her. Her father, I knew, was a Brigadier (retd), and her mother too looked an average member of the upper middle class. Both had polite vacant smiles fixed uneasily to their faces, and they appeared in every way too mundane and ordinary to have bred so exotic a creature as the shimmering bride before them.

She circulated through the room with an assured catlike grace. One mehndied hand carelessly held on to, horror of horrors, a glass of gin! The other was graciously bestowed on B.R., who followed in her wake, a slightly glazed look in his fine eyes.

They came to the corner where I stood. A paternal Rai Bahadur again hovered around me. At the sight of B.R. my heart, my stomach, my legs, all turned to unset jelly. He was sweating profusely and a lock of hair was plastered at an odd angle across his forehead. His eyes had a strange expression, glassy yet triumphant, like a hunter displaying an unusually fine kill. And yet, upon seeing me, his expression changed to one of warmth, of penetration, of special communication. 'This is Priya, darling,' he said enthusiastically, and to my mind, a shade patronisingly. 'One of the – no, the, most beautiful and intelligent girl in our office.' He didn't bother to introduce Paro to me.

We made quite a cosy little family group. Uneasily, I tried to make my escape, but Paro seemed to have sensed the undercurrents of intimacy and shared experience. Her eyes narrowed in a look that would, later, warn me to be on my guard. She inspected the length and breadth of me, the wilting hibiscus, the stained red chiffon, the tawdry gold sandals.

'Lovely to meet you, Priya,' she said, and moved on, bored, to the next group of people.

The workers from the factory came late, as B.R. did not hold with corporate productivity suffering for parties and private celebrations. The foreman presented her with a huge bouquet of flowers on behalf of all the workers, who stood gaping at her in awe and admiration. She examined the bouquet critically, even a little distastefully, and then extracted two white rosebuds which she then carefully pinned on to her chignon.

'Bubu', she said throatily, 'there are flowers and flowers, you know.' Then she bent to whisper something in his quiescent ear; and I decided that I hated her.

Rai Bahadur was by now becoming a positive nuisance. He had already recounted several suggestive jokes, and now he was telling me about how much he missed his wife, and how, if she hadn't died, he wouldn't have had to worry about his only son so much and what a responsibility it was.

Thankfully, dinner was soon announced. Some of the staff had insisted on a wedding cake, so B.R. had to slice a three-tiered pink and white masterpiece of the confectioner's art. He cut through it tidily with a knife swathed in pink and white ribbon, then grabbed the little bridegroom perched upon the tumbling cake and placed him tenderly in Paro's waiting mouth. She smiled, and winked mischievously. Loud clapping broke out, and my carefully suppressed jealousy overpowered me. Bearers rushed in to dismantle the remaining edifice and distribute it to the waiting staff. Mary and Ivy oohed and aahed loudly at everything; everyone dug away at the cake as though it were manna from heaven. Nauseated, I stumbled out, somehow pushing my way across the press of people, all on their way to the laden dining-tables.

I clattered home on the lonely suburban train. Dadar . . . Mahim . . . Vile Parle . . . Each station seemed like an incantation against love, hope, faith. Finally, the train reached Andheri, and I got off, tired, hungry and miserable. Walking home from the station, I bought a banana from a thelawala, and threw the peel across the hedge into the neighbouring building. When I reached home I was myself again.

Mother was lying on her cot, coughing asthmatically. (The Bombay climate didn't suit her.) Bhaiya was glued to the radio, listening to 'A Date with You'. As the music billowed across the room where we all slept, I watched my mother fiddling with her scanty hair, and wondered what Paro would look like after fifteen years. Spitefully, but with some accuracy, I assured myself that she would run to fat.

Gradually, she became an obsession for me. Subconsciously I would find myself mouthing her words; phrases that were not mine would spill unsuspecting from my lips; gestures that were hers would enact themselves in involuntary mime. For example, I too would throw back my head in a deep throaty laugh, and my eyes would narrow in a pale shadow of her piercing gaze.

Not that I ever had much opportunity to meet her. She often flitted in and out of the office at lunchtimes, loaded with expensive shopping, dressed in crisp white cotton saris and high white sandals, with white flowers in her slightly frizzy hair. All of us would get up and smile nicely at her. She would utterly disregard our servile attentions and walk straight into B.R.'s office, leaving a trail of expensive perfume behind her.

My fingers, busy on the keyboard, would tremble in rage. Once home, I would lie under the blue floral Bombay Dyeing coverlets, and dream about them to the rhythms of my mother's quiet snores and Atul's adenoidal wheeze. I could picture him slowly undressing her; my breath would quicken as he held each firm white breast in his long brutal fingers; I could see the glazed look in his eyes as he sat astride her. Somewhere, our roles would be transposed and I would become her, and feel a triumphant power in his climax, and arrive myself at heaven's gates, to the feverish clutch of my index finger. My mother, stumbling in the dark on her way to the bathroom, would ask me grumpily why I was still awake.

Variations of this fantasy overcame me almost every night. I would awake disoriented in our small all-purpose hall-cum-dining-room, suffused with shame and contempt for the poverty and meanness around me. I would vow to rise from that mire; I would dream of grace, of beauty, and harmony, and I would resolve to

13

brush my hair a hundred strokes every night before I slept.

Then Anita, B.R.'s secretary, became engaged to be married. It was an arranged match and her husband did not want her to continue working. B.R. elected me from the typists' pool to become his secretary. So I bade goodbye to Mary and Ivy and became one of the twice-born. I had to do the flowers in his office (I bought a book on Ikebana) and I had to answer his calls. She would telephone him every fifteen minutes on any possible pretext, and often he would instruct me to tell her he was not in, or that he was busy in a meeting. Those would be my fleeting moments of golden revenge; I would picture her, thwarted and vexed, and bask in my power.

I also grew adept at drafting and independent correspondence. We manufactured sewing machines: Sita Sewing Machines were, in fact, synonymous in those halcyon Sixties with domesticity, matrimony and family life. B.R. was a meticulous businessman, an exacting perfectionist, and almost the nervous housewife in his finicky adherence to routine and detail. He had also, I am told, a near-genius for marketing, and the company, founded by his father, flourished under his tender ministrations. He was forever wooing the Market, visiting agents, distributors, 'wheeling about,' as he wryly put it, 'to charm the Dealers to do the dealing.'

He had been away for almost a week on one such sales promotion tour, and there were several urgent papers pending his signature. I decided to take the papers with me personally and leave them at his residence on my way home, for him to sign and approve so that I could forward them the next day. Becoming B.R.'s secretary had given a new dimension to my self-confidence, and it was quite without trepidation that I trilled the doorbell on that pseudo-antique mahogany door. A starched and beturbanned bearer answered my ring. I could well have left the papers with him; but the urge to use this pretext to observe her on home territory overtook me.

She was sitting on the balcony, slightly sweaty in the mid-afternoon miasma. The westerly sun cast a hypnotic reflected glare, and she sat dreaming, her creamy, pink-nail-polished feet curled idly on the chair. Her hair was slightly frizzy with the humidity, and she was leafing limply through the pages of a foreign magazine. She was quite unaware of my scrutiny, and I stared spellbound for a while until the bearer gave a polite cough, to indicate my arrival, which shook the fan of his starched white turban ever so slightly.

She looked up, her grey-green eyes crinkling into their familiar stare.

'Some papers for Sir,' I stammered.

'What papers?' she asked suspiciously. 'Sit down, have some tea.'

With that, she dismissed the turbanned slave, who had, in all probability, been sent off to see a film on the day of my previous and only visitation. I explained, and showed her the papers. 'You're a North Indian, aren't you?' she enquired next. 'You're Priya Sharma,' this almost accusingly.

'My father was from Rajasthan, but we've always lived in Bombay…'

'Oh,' she said indifferently. I could not tell if she approved or otherwise of Rajasthan, or for that matter of Bombay.

Critically, and even a little competitively, she sized me up. Missing nothing, she took in my white cotton sari, my high white sandals, my white plastic purse.

'Aren't you the girl who wore the red flower in her hair, that day?' she asked suddenly. Looking back, today, I can say that perhaps it was only the cruelty of arrogant youth; but then, in that moment, in the present of that hot mid-afternoon, I reeled at the sudden strident cruelty. 'Yes,' I answered shamefacedly, wishing the earth would swallow me up, and swallow my white sandals and my white home-starched Lucknowi sari too.

Just then, the doorbell rang again. The waiter came in with a tea-tray, suddenly looking comically self-important. 'Sahib has come,' he announced solemnly, and yet with a certain festive joy, as when a king returns and courtiers reassemble in jubilation. Paro got up, looking vexed, and then without a word to me she disappeared into the azure air-conditioned silence.

I sat alone and sipped the tea, which had come on a large silver tray with a starched matte tea-cloth embroidered in cross-stitch with pink roses. Such tea-cloths I meticulously stitched and embroidered for my trousseau – and just so I tried, in the early years of my marriage, to serve tea to my husband when he returned from the law-courts.

16

The bearer came again, and told me magisterially that Sahib had asked me to wait. I waited, obediently, in the comfortable cane chair, lost in reveries of just such a life. I awoke from the daydream to find the sun about to be swallowed by the blood-red sea, and the *Woman and Homes* and the *Filmfares* flapping agitatedly in the evening breeze. The plants in the balcony had begun to awaken slowly to the night, and the soft smells of Chameli and Raat-ki-Rani wafted over the petrol fumes of the evening traffic.

I had waited for over an hour, and was about to leave when they appeared. They were both freshly showered and bathed. She was wearing a very low-cut sleeveless blouse, which had practically no back and which almost took my breath away by its daring, and a plain russet sari. A gold Kamardhani hung provocatively from her slender waist. She looked like a cat that has had all the cream. He, too, wore an expression of self-satisfaction. They exuded the civet smell of recent sexual activity.

Since I really had nothing much to say to him, I handed over the papers and left for home. All the way to Andheri, past Dadar, Mahim and Vile Parle, I sat brooding on nothing.

There was a visible change of atmosphere at home. The room was still the same fifteen feet by twenty; it still housed the same divan-cum-beds at one end, and the same precarious table with the four even more precarious dining chairs at the other. The little temple on the table next to my mother's bed was, however, today redolent with incense, and agarbatti droppings bespattered the small Hanuman, poised with Mountain in hand to take off to Ramchandraji's aid. The glum framed photograph of my deceased father was also garlanded. The radio with its crotcheted cover and crown of plastic flowers was, as ever, tuned to Radio Ceylon, but the pall of depression that normally crept like gloam-dust into our house was absent. There was, indeed, an uncertain festive air about the place.

My mother, who was busy cooking in the little balcony-cum-kitchen, rushed out upon hearing me.

'Priya, Priya beti, ek khushkhabari hai...' she said theatrically. Then, predictibly, she burst into unabashed sobs; I sat, perplexed, until her sobs subsided. Presently she began tenderly to stroke my hair. 'Kitni sundar dulhan banegi,' she said, holding my chin in her work-hardened hands, and looking long and tenderly into my eyes until I winced with pain.

Slowly it dawned upon me. I had received an offer of marriage.

She was quite incoherent with excitement, and it was some time before I could extract even the basic facts from her. Apparently, her sister in Meerut had written to ask if I was agreeable to meeting her (her sister's) husband's nephew, who was a lawyer in Delhi, and from a prosperous and decent family. With trembling hands she extracted the letter from under her pillow and read out in an All India Radio announcer's voice, 'He (the boy) is of sober and decent habits and is likely to have good prospects. His height is five feet five inches, and

18

he is a little plump, but very fair and handsome. He is also of very good nature, and I would be very happy to have Priya as the Lakshmi in my sister-in-law's already prosperous house.' A photograph also spilled out, of an owlish youth leaning on a Standard Herald car.

The car decided me. From then on I was caught in a whirl of feverish planning and anticipation; all before I had even encountered my future husband-to-be, or he had met or approved me.

My photograph was, of course, duly taken at a studio and dispatched to him, as was a resumé of my many skills and talents. He found fault with neither, and within a week we had got together the requisite clothes, jewellery and associated paraphernalia of marriage.

When I told them at the office, they all asked excitedly, 'Is it Arranged or Love?' When I told them it was Arranged they all looked a little disappointed.

My marriage was a middle-class one, much as any other. We did not have many relatives, and so it was uneventful, even a little boring. My husband was a virgin, and did not seem to notice that I was not. B.R. accepted my resignation with equanimity. They could not attend the wedding, which was in May, as they were holidaying in Europe that summer. I received a Sita Sewing Machine as an official wedding gift, and B.R. and Paro sent a cut-glass vase as a personal present.

We went to Nainital for our honeymoon. Suresh unburdened all his ambitions, his hopes and dreams, to me. He wanted to prove himself, to make it. Now that I was his wife, he wanted to ensure for me every possible happiness that he could provide. He even told me that I was beautiful; but it sounded foolish from his lips, although I was flattered.

Sometimes, I would think of B.R. and my heart would sigh. But my head told me that I had not got such a bad deal after all.

Suresh had a two-bedroom rented flat in Delhi; he was very sociable and entertained regularly. I waded laboriously through cookbooks while he sat reading his briefs, and soon mastered the basic rudiments and skills of Continental, Moghlai and Chinese cooking. At night, we would grapple with our sexual appetites. I filled the balcony of the first-floor flat with a profusion of potted plants, which I tended with an almost religious fervour. I would spend the afternoons there sipping at my tea and leafing through magazines. Every now and then I would come across a photograph of Paro in the social columns of the *Onlooker* or *Eve's Weekly*. She seemed to have become quite a luminary in the Bombay social scene. Fashion shows in aid of war-widows, charity premières for spastics, jam-sessions and fetes for worthy causes, she was prominent in all of them. I would scrutinise her photographs with special care. She was looking as sensual as ever, but she had become heavier. I must confess that even my spider's eye could find no further flaws.

And then the monsoons came, and during the thunderous rain-drenched nights our relationship even burgeoned into something approaching love. In the hot muggy mornings, however, things looked quite different again. Suresh across the dining table at breakfast was groggy, insensitive, and not, let me face it, cut of the cloth of Romance. Which is not to say that we were not happy.

Suresh took me with him to Bombay once. He had a case there and I was to stay on at my mother's for a while. The day the case was over we went for dinner to the Taj to celebrate. We sat late, lingering over our coffee. As we were leaving, I spied her entering, probably on her way to the nightclub for a late dinner.

They were in a group, and did not notice me. I too was slightly embarrassed at the prospect of a confrontation, and did not go forward to say hello. She was wearing a black sequinned off-shoulder kurta, which left one shoulder completely bare, almost naked to my prudish eyes. She was staggering slightly, and leaning for support on the arm of a very handsome young man. B.R., meanwhile, was in deep and earnest conversation with a plump and not very pretty girl. His eyes held the gleam of conquest. They departed in a whiff of perfume and gaiety, while we took a cab back to my mother's familiar Andheri flat.

I returned to Delhi within a week. My mother was still the same, except that she had developed a filmi mother's wracking cough; although my brother was studying medicine he seemed quite unconcerned about it. It was one of the various small grievances with which she would constantly nag him, now that I was no longer on the horizon for the purpose. She would go on and on about the necessity to get him married and bring home a nice bahu to look after her in her declining years.

Bhaiyya took it all in his stride, for he had been nagged as long as I could remember and was too phlegmatic to ever react. Actually, her nagging about the cough was quite justified, for it was T.B. that she died of, four years later. It was diagnosed only after her death, thus depriving her of the certain bitter satisfaction she could have extracted from this neglect.

Delhi seemed like heaven after that week of maternal recriminations. We had light Scandinavian furniture in our flat, and I had copied a painting by Picasso in oils and had it framed in the drawing-room. Once a week I went to the beauty parlour to get my hair set; I wore a lacquered bouffant, with either a small chignon or a high pony-tail. My hair today is still frizzy from all that maltreatment, but at the time it gave me some sorely needed social confidence. I tried to take up smoking, but Suresh would have none of it, and even tried to restrain me from wearing anything but saris. I quickly retreated back into my Indian wife image, but I was watching and learning.

I realised that my only weapon in an indifferent world was Suresh, and I decided to groom him patiently until my ministrations bore dividends. We short-listed the thirty or so people in the legal and allied professions who could be useful to us, and along with a smattering of friends (for Suresh was a very friendly man, a natural extrovert), started hosting regular informal get-togethers at home. Suresh affected a bluff good humour, and would offer himself quite without rancour as joker, buffoon and spittoon to his social and economic superiors.

This assiduous and intensive programme of cultivation could not but pay off, and so we were soon part of a smart young set of people, not of the first water, admittedly, but putting on a brave front of gaiety and good times. All the women looked like me, some better, many worse. Every weekend there would be a get-together somewhere; over beer or whisky, cigarette smoke and ghazals, we would try excitedly to keep abreast of the changing world. Then we would leave, on our scooters and in our cars, for our separate homes and houses. Yet it was not camaraderie that bound us together, only an intense competitiveness.

I remember how, one evening, at a pot-luck party, we got to discussing the jet-set – Bombay's rich – whom we pretended to despise or at least be indifferent to. A journalist's wife, whose parents were from Bombay, told us of a party she had been to.

'You can't imagine,' she insisted, her eyes big as saucers, 'what these types behave like! There's this guy – I've forgotten his name but his wife is this dame Paro. They're stinking rich and she's really beautiful. They have these wild parties where everybody – but everybody – who is anybody is invited. Bunny, of course, is a good friend of theirs. Well, he's really very charming, but I think she's a bitch! You must meet them sometime.'

Suresh's interest was aroused. He really had become hideously obvious. I could sense him smelling out a possible contact, or client.

'Arrey, they're very good friends of Priya's,' he claimed importantly. 'She worked in his firm for a long time; and that cut-glass vase in our drawing-room – they gave it to us at our wedding.' So Bannerjee and he decided to invite B.R. over the next time he was in Delhi. Of course, the invitation never materialised, and it was only many years later that I glimpsed them again.

So it is that I am sitting here, many years later, still grappling with these visitations from the past. I am still trying to lay their ghosts, banish their tyrannical mythologies; it is to be a therapeutic experience, an old-fashioned catharsis, an enema. I shall vomit out my malice and envy and adoration.

'You know, Priya, you used to look so ghastly then,' she would say complacently, and I would hug the warm almost-forgotten secret of B.R.'s fleeting love.

This is the Paro who is but recently liberated from marriage and convention; she is still convinced that she is as young and desirable as she ever was. Her massive breasts, like the enlarged pores of her skin, have grown ponderous with age. Even her fingers have become fatter – but this coarsening of the body has also somehow catalysed a startling vitality of mind, a vigour that is as crude as it is real. Life has not tired her – she is undiminished, she has grown. She is still obsessed, loudly and clamorously, with questions that the rest of us answered, or decided not to answer, at some period around adolescence.

Women's liberation isn't so chic any more, it has become a little dated, even irrelevant, like Trade-unionism to Socialism, as Lenin would say. Fashionable Women aren't liberated any more; it's all morchas and placards and sweaty types shouting about dowry and

24

bride-burning. Paro has done it all, she's left a husband and a lover, she has a small son of ambiguous parentage. She is a conversation piece at dinner parties, and it is considered daring and chic to know her. And she is, or thinks she is, my best friend.

It was at a dinner party at the 'Tabela' that we met, some five years ago. We had gone to the discotheque with a friend (a client really), and she was sitting at the next table. The client insisted on introducing us; I was afraid she wouldn't remember me. And she didn't.

'I used to work in your husband's office,' I said formally; then realised that he wasn't her husband any more.

We joined them at their table. 'He used to be my husband,' she said. She sounded quite unconcerned. Then, about half an hour later, she burst into a massive horselaugh. (She had downed four large whiskies.) 'You're the one with the hibiscus!' she said, choking on her whisky sour. 'The one with the hibiscus!'

She had left B.R. only six months before. Everybody was talking about it. She was living in open adulterous sin with 'Bucky' Bhandpur, test cricketer and scion of a princely family. The 'Bucky', I gathered, was in commemoration of his faintly protruding front teeth, which lent a strange charm to his lean face. He was, like B.R., what the boys in the office used to call 'A Known Romeo'. He was also a little younger than her.

He didn't appear to be terribly enamoured of her that night – in fact, when I bent down under the table to retrieve my handbag, I found amorous foot-play in progress between him and the young and glamorous model who was sitting beside me. And then they left together soon after. We offered to drop Paro home, and as we steered uncertainly through the steaming heat of the summer night, we found that 'Bucky' Bhandpur and his model had crashed their long flashy yellow sportscar into a family of three who were crossing the road near the bus-stop on Zakir Hussain Marg.

They were villagers from Gurgaon, a farmer and his wife and their young son. Luckily no one seemed to be hurt. They all were safe, Bhandpur and the model and the pedestrians. But the mandatory crowd had gathered; His Highness seemed quite fazed by the alcohol and the heat, and the young model was shrinking into herself at the collective comments of the crowd, who seemed more obsessed, lewdly and vocally, with her tiny halter top than by the fate of the terrified peasant family.

The mood of the janata was fast turning ugly. Paro showed her true mettle then; she got out of the car, into the thick of the crowd, and looked things over. When she realised that there was nothing much the matter, she clapped her hands, memsahib fashion.

'Jao, Jao' she said peremptorily. 'Ab tamasha khatam.' Then she extracted five hundred-rupee notes from her purse, and handed them to the woman, whose wailing and accusations immediately stopped. 'Jao,' she said to the crowd, once again, and miraculously they dispersed. 'Get into the back seat,' she snapped at the model.

The terrified creature did as she was told. Paro got into the driver's seat, and without so much as a bye-

bye to us they whizzed off into the dark night. As my husband fumbled with the ignition keys, something between a leer and a salute shone in his eyes.

'What a woman!' he exclaimed, in sincere admiration.

Soon after that, she left 'Bucky' Bhandpur as well. She was facing a number of legal problems. There were cases filed against her by her landlord, by her against her tenants, some problems regarding her father's will and death duties, about her divorce, her alimony. Every relationship and encounter seemed to have ended in bitterness, misunderstanding and wrangling. Suresh gallantly entered the fray, and, most uncharacteristically for him, offered to do all her cases free. He justified this by saying that he was using her 'contacts' for leverage. But I suspect he was more than a little enamoured of her. Surprisingly, this fact caused me no jealousy; in fact, I felt a certain complacent pleasure at the thought that it was now she who needed my husband.

I exulted in my kindness, and would constantly and insistently call her over for lunches and dinners. We have no children, so although I am very houseproud I do not really have much to do all day. She would come and sit for hours on end. All afternoon we would loll about the living-room divan, and she would talk on, compulsively, about herself, always herself. Compulsively, I would listen. She never asked me anything about myself and I in turn never ventured to tell.

★

'He raped me in a grove of pine-trees,' she said, tears

in her eyes. 'He sodomised me in the woods behind the chapel. I still have the water-colour I was painting when that happened; it shows the landscape exactly as it was the day my life began to get fucked up. You know, birds, butterflies, blue skies, the works. It hangs in my bedroom. I look at it and weep.'

I listened agape. Differentiating between fact and fiction was always a problem with Paro. But there were tears in her eyes.

'I was the only child of middle-aged parents,' she continued. 'I was a bother in their well-ordered lives. Besides, they were in the army, and kept getting transferred and things. I spent my whole life in a boarding school in the hills.'

'Lucky you,' I said fervently.

'I was good. You know, I was the head girl in my final year. Man, I wanted to be P.M. of India, you know.'

I nodded in understanding.

'But we had this art master – Marcus something. I loved painting, you know. I was good at it. I suppose I was very sexy-looking for a schoolgirl. Anyway, there I was, busy with my landscape, trying to get the right cerulean blue for the sky and the fucking Vandyke brown for the trees. It was during the Dussehra vacations. My folks were abroad so I stayed back at the hostel. There was no one else around. He was quite young, this art master, and very good-looking in a long-haired way. Anyway, he tells me, "You look like a wood nymph." Then he starts getting sexy… you know… and I don't know what's happening but I sort of like it. And then suddenly he's on top of me, right there in between all those pine needles, and fucking me right and left. And there are crows going "Caw, Caw" in the trees. After a while I liked it. I liked it one hell of a lot.' She chuckled softly. But I could sense some pain.

'After that, we were at it, wherever and whenever we could. I thought I was in love with him. Actually, half the girls in the class were. One day I wrote him a letter. There was this girl in my class...' Suddenly her eyes narrowed. 'Actually she looked a lot like you. She was in love with him too. She found this letter, and took it to the headmistress.' She was silent for a while.

'What happened next?' I asked.

'Well, this headmistress came looking for me that night. He was in my room. I had a room to myself. I was the head girl, you know. All hell broke loose. I was expelled. I told them that I loved him but they didn't find that funny. He said I had led him on. It seems he had already got the ayah pregnant. They had hushed that up.'

She laughed bitterly. 'Well, man, nobody could hush this up. The shit really hit the ceiling. It was in the papers and all. Head girl raped. Public school morality. Letters to the editor and all that. My parents went out of their minds. My father retired early because he said he couldn't bear the scandal. We shifted to Delhi. Things were pretty quiet for a while.'

Her grey-green eyes crinkled in memory. 'Then, in college, I met Bubu... Man, did he fall for me like a ton of bricks! His father sent a proposal. Apparently, they hadn't heard about my rape-scene. Funny thing is that I wasn't raped, I loved every moment of it. Anyway, Daddyji was so glad to get Bubu off his hands that he didn't bother to scrutinise the police record too carefully. Maybe if I had a ma-in-law she would have been more careful. And so there it was. Marriage.' She paused. 'I always knew it sounded too good to last. And it didn't.' She was silent.

'You know, I read somewhere that most women marry the best provider they can stomach. That wasn't my scene at all.'

That wasn't all we talked about. We exchanged schoolgirl confidences. She taught me how to apply eye makeup. She would go on about love, sex, cooking, or anything else that caught her fancy. She taught me how to make garlic bread. Her irreverence both frightened and exhilarated me. She could decimate people with a mere sentence, and she used her mocking wit as adeptly as a sharp little scorpion. She was, of course, a Scorpio. She would talk agitatedly about Red Indians and the injustice being done to them. (She was in love with Marlon Brando.)

'But, Paro,' I would argue logically, 'what about the Harijans?'

'But Marlon Brando is too Sa-a-xy, yaar,' she would reply, drawling out the word in a way that held me spellbound.

She did not perceive the shame and furtiveness of sex. She talked of mating her bitch and the complexities of her own sexual life with the same directness and with the same degree of involvement.

Matter-of-factly, she told me the length of each of her lovers' organs.

She made me laugh.

She dismissed B.R.'s new wife (he had just re-married), with a languid 'That Ayah! What yaar!' Of her ex-father-inlaw, the Rai Bahadur: 'That old lech! Thank God he's dead.'

She was flattered by my curiosity and attention. She would mock me gently, with overtones of friendship. I in turn was flattered by her laughter. I think I was in love with her.

'You had a real pash for my Bubu, didn't you?' she would ask indulgently. 'Your Suresh is a good man,' she would conclude sagely, after tearing everyone she knew to tatters.

Her fatal flaw was vanity. She loved self-dramatisation. I sometimes wondered what she would be like, alone in an empty room; whether she would simply go limp and collapse, or posture and practise for her next encounter.

She loved her body and cried like a baby at the slightest physical hurt. Yet once she drew blood and wrote her name with it on a novel to prove to me that she was not afraid of pain.

She was, of course, an indifferent mother.

What did she live off? How did she survive? I asked curiously.

'Stocks, shares, family property – the occasional sale of some jewellery,' she replied airily. 'And, of course, Bubu settled some property on me after our marriage.

The rent is enough for my simple needs.'

'But is that right? I mean, you left him, don't you feel funny using his money?' I would persist.

'Look, sweetie,' she would say, her eyes darkening, 'they made the rules.'

When I was in school, in nursery, we had a bad girl in our class. She was not allowed to sit with the other children (we sat in a circle around the teacher). The bad girl sat alone, like a spaceship in lonely orbit, right next to the teacher; and in my mind she assumed a strange and terrible power. Timidly, I tried to befriend her, and share the lunch my mother packed for me with her. She would trample my parathas underfoot and grind them into the dust with her sandals. I would never tell my mother, nor complain to the teacher. Paro exercised the same irresistible attraction for me.

My servants adored her. 'Asli Memsahib hai,' they would say fervently.

'The story of my life…?' he would muse. 'Here I am, in the middle years, *entre deux guerres*, twenty years largely wasted…' He smiled enigmatically, one eyebrow arching slightly in an affectation that still set my nerves atingle. 'T.S. Eliot,' he amplified. 'How is Paro, incidentally? I believe she is a great friend of yours now. I must say, you look as pretty as ever, Priya. In fact, more so than ever.' All this in his best Panjabi Oxford accent, which he was as vain about as his Oxford Panjabi accent; 'One must never underestimate the vernacular, y'know…'

We were sitting in the Harbour Bar in the Bombay Taj – my successful lawyer husband, myself, B.R.'s well-maintained and dutiful wife, and B.R. himself, richer and more articulate than ever, but running to flab, both mentally and physically. His proud and valiant bearing had deteriorated, to the spider eyes of my fierce, dormant first love, into a self-concerned vanity. His new wife, who sat beside him in a loose chiffon butterfly kaftan, was without doubt the most utterly vacuous woman I had ever met. Her presence was completely negative; perhaps she was an antidote to Paro's excessive greedy vitality.

It was strange, for she had by any standards a stunning figure, and there was a certain pretty charm to her fair dimpled face, and yet her eyes held a blankness that was sheer and terrifying. She was a black hole of grasping malignant dependency. B.R. hated her; that much was obvious in the controlled effort of his speech; and she loved him.

It had become a real joke with their fat-cat friends, this traumatic wrenching of marriages that was accelerating into an even more frenetic marital musical chairs. B.R. had married Bubbles on the rebound just six months after Paro left him, and already he was flaunting his mistresses through Bombay's cloistered social circles.

Presently, the insistent pressure of his foot reached me. I responded cautiously, and remained in a frenzy of hope and expectation until he telephoned me the next day.

He called me for dinner soon after. Suresh was already back in Delhi. I told Bhaiyya that I was meeting some of my old office friends, which was after all true in a way.

B.R. asked me to come directly to his flat. Bubbles had gone to Poona, to her parents.

He was waiting for me when I arrived. I sat awkwardly while he poured me a drink. There was silence all around. 'Priya, my love,' he said finally, 'you are looking as beautiful as ever. Marriage seems to suit you.' He sighed. 'I've missed you, you know.' He seemed to mean it.

My petticoat was already wet with anticipation. But he didn't touch me. He wasn't looking so debonair any more; his eyes were troubled; he kept pouring himself drink after drink. 'I really missed you,' he said again. My sherry wasn't tasting so heady anymore. This wasn't the B.R. that I knew. Or loved.

We were sitting in his bedroom. The bedroom where Paro had lived, and Bubbles. It looked just as before, as neutral as any hotel room.

Suddenly he got up and walked to the dressing table. He opened a drawer and pulled out a photograph album; an untidy heap of photographs spilled out. They were not all yellowed with age. He handed me one of them. A thin young man with rather intense eyes stared out. It was B.R. I was shocked at how thin he had been. And how young his eyes.

'That was me,' he said unnecessarily. 'When I was up at Oxford.' He shuffled through the photographs. 'And that was my girlfriend. She taught me a lot. But she died in a car-crash.' I was curious, and stared hard, trying to fathom, beyond this girl with her hands in her trouser-pockets and her dated hairstyle, the B.R. she had known.

He fished out another one, of a play in progress.

There was a young man, a boy almost, with a skull in his hand. 'That's Keith,' he said. 'He was my best friend. He committed suicide.'

'All your friends seem to have died,' I said, trying to sound jocular, and failing.

'But I continue,' he replied, 'living and partly living.' Suddenly he was animated again. 'I hated Oxford,' he said emphatically, 'and I hate India as well. My father forced Oxford upon me. He thought it was the ultimate status symbol. But my mother didn't want me to go. She was very real.' His eyes grew soft. 'As you are,' he said, and bent over to kiss me.

We moved to the bed, and he entered me. He lavished so much tenderness upon me that I was overwhelmed with gratitude. I wouldn't have minded dying in those moments of perfect bliss.

Just then there was a loud bang. The air-conditioner had fused. We continued, but the room soon became unbearably warm. 'Let's shift to the guest room,' he said.

It was past midnight when he stopped for a cigarette. We were sweating even in the air-conditioned cool. An oblong of light fell into the dark room from the open bathroom door. As he puffed at the cigarette, I glimpsed his sad eyes. An unutterable sadness enveloped me; I did not ever want such joy to end.

'B.R.,' I said, 'I don't ever want to leave you.' I clung to him. His skin was as soft and tender as a boiled egg after it has been peeled.

He switched on the light. 'Post-coital sadness,' he said. I savoured the word. 'Let's get pre-coital again,' he laughed. But there was still some sadness in his eyes.

Later we indulged in some post-coital conversation. 'I should never have married Paro,' he said. 'It wasn't me she wanted. It was the fixtures and fittings that came with me. She hurt me by trying to use me.'

Paro was my friend. Involuntarily I rose to her defence. 'Perhaps you hurt her too,' I said, 'by all your womanising.' I bit my tongue, and blushed, for it was in the circumstances a rather incongruous statement. But he seemed not to have noticed.

'Men are very insecure creatures,' he said. 'They need a lot of love. And they need beautiful women.' He laughed bitterly. 'Unfortunately beautiful women are seldom designed to provide love.' And he held me close and made love to me again.

Did I feel no twinge of guilt in so betraying Paro? That question is strange in itself, for Paro was no longer his wife, and had taken many lovers since. Yet to my confused mind they were both irrevocably wedded, twin deities like the sun and the moon.

I told Suresh I wanted to spend another month in Bombay with Dolly Bhabhi, who was expecting her first child. Bhaiyya lived in a large flat now, gifted to him by his parents-in-law. I would meet B.R. almost every evening, and have dinner with him, with wine, candlelight, roses and all the other trappings of a covert romance. We would make love in anonymous hotel rooms. I would punctuate his appointments and draft short memos of passion in his absences. We would copulate with a love that was both urgent and tender; he would examine every pore and crevice of my body with the wonder of a treasure that has been washed back from the sea. But unlike Paro, he would rarely talk, and never again about himself. Yet, perhaps, he was, through me, talking to her, telling her something, as in a letter that has been put out to sea in a bottle.

It was a second youth, a middle-aged revival of dreams. I had indeed never even dreamt of such passion, and I kept delaying the inevitable return to Delhi and Suresh's clumsy hateful arms. I was outliving my welcome with Dolly Bhabhi, who seemed, in her uncertain accent, always on the verge of a sarcastic remark about her 'Ultra Smart' sister-in-law, invariably concluding with unhealthy malice that she (bhabhi) was after all a simple housewife and not qualified to pass judgement, but what Suresh bhai sahib would say she did not know...

But Bombay held me in thrall. Those were perhaps the happiest days of my life. B.R. never mentioned Paro again. Nor did he ever talk about his incumbent wife, Bubbles. All he would do was quote poetry, and sigh, running his fingers dreamily through his thinning hair. And, of course, make love to me.

Sex had become, to him, more than a sport, it was a duty, a vocation, a calling. I sensed that it was with sex alone that he reached out to the world, and it was with sex that he shut out thought, emotion and feeling. Women could, perhaps, sense this immense sexual generosity, and came to him for succour and healing. And he allowed himself to be used as a lamp-post, or as a letterbox for women to send messages to their husbands through. I do not think he ever refused a woman; it was as though he were bound, by his code of honour, to ravish every female that he encountered. I think in a curious way he needed me. The habit of servility was of course ingrained in me, and B.R. had of course been my boss. It was not long, nevertheless, before our adultery ran its course.

We were to meet at his house one evening. Bubbles was still in Poona, with her parents. Upon my arrival I found a dishevelled-looking B.R. seated in uneasy conversation with a beauteous female. She looked very tense, on the edge of hysteria, in fact. On seeing me she got even more agitated. Suspicion rose in my mind like a foul weed. I tried to drown it but I knew, in my heart of hearts, that our time was up.

We sipped at some wine together in rigid silence. 'Well, I'll make a move,' she said, finally. As she bent down to strap on her sandals, which were strewn angrily before her, she let out a shrill sound. 'My payals... my payals...' she shrieked, almost accusingly, and started hunting frenziedly through the room for her payals, in what appeared to me to be the most unlikely and impossible places. She threw a mess of magazines and papers about her, and angrily hurled away the little embroidered cushions from the settee. She ferreted, like an angry Pekinese, under the delicate gilt sofa, and sniffed under the corner table, her luscious behind looking suggestive, if not obscene, as she crouched on all fours, her sari pallav tied round her waist, her hair flying loose from its carefully tended French roll. Finally, she emerged triumphant with an excited yelp from under the sofa, a gold anklet clasped in her lilywhite hands. She had ransacked and quite devastated the room.

'Gold…' she panted. 'Real gold… we are from Royal Family, you know.' And with that she flounced out of the room.

I fixed an unblinking stare on B.R., hoping to shame him into confession. Wearily, mechanically, he edged towards me and held on to my obliging breast in a preoccupied manner. He breathed heavily, a caveman trying to revive a dying fire, and moaned and duly went through all the motions and simulations of passion; but he couldn't manage an erection. He seemed shamed and shattered by this inadequacy, and began flailing about wildly, and attacked me with even greater ferocity. Soon we were hinged; only, at the moment of orgasm, there was a distinct and embarrassing sound, like a motorcycle starting. He coughed quickly to cover up, and then both of us sat in silence again.

We went out for dinner after that, to a restaurant facing the sea. There were rows of beggars lining the footpath, all standing on tiptoe and attempting to peep through the hedges and the tinted glass at the glory within.

Jealousy and love were darting through the weeds in my mind. We sat in treacherous, betrayed silence, me examining the menu card and B.R. lost in moody thought.

Suddenly there was a faint buzzing in my ears, and I sensed rather than felt a presence in the other end of the room. It was Paro. She was dressed in a black gown and in the dark of the restaurant she looked very like the Paro of long ago, as though summoned from a dream. She saw us immediately upon entering and advanced towards our table with unremitting, unhesitating directness, her escort forgotten. Soon she stood directly above us, like a figure from a play, her white arms with their faint down shining in the candlelight, her hands by her side, tightly clenched in anger.

'Well, this is a surprise,' she said. 'My husband and his secretary are at it again. Only, I thought, Priya, that you were my friend.' Then she looked B.R. straight in the eye, her glittering lashes coated with gold and black and venom, and spat, with force and accuracy, into his startled face. B.R. was devastated. He shrank, crumpled, and did not even pretend to recover. We spent the rest of the evening in strained, distracted thought, cowering under her malignant presence. Paro had seated herself directly across from us and was eating and drinking with great gusto. Every now and then she would fix a look of contempt and hatred in our direction, and then smile brightly at the young man with her.

He looked young enough to be her son. He was a thin youth in a white kurta-pyjama, with a straggly beard, and an ethereal look, and looked a sort of oriental Jesus Christ with a faintly obese Mary Magdalen. When they had finished and got up to leave, there was a slight tussle about who would pay the bill. Paro paid. B.R. and I sat crouched in our corner, admonished and afraid; not once did it strike us that she was not his wife. Although we had long finished our food and coffee, we left only a safe five minutes after they had departed.

We drove aimlessly around Marine Drive after that. We sat primly apart. There was a faint monsoon drizzle, and the steady susurration of the sea at ebb tide. After a while B.R. parked the car, and proceeded to stare at me keenly, his hands still on the steering. Then he leaned forward to kiss me, but barely had our lips met than some villainous-looking characters loomed outside the window glass, gesturing and knocking threateningly. B.R.'s immediate reflex was panic; he snapped the lock shut, switched on the ignition, and speeded away, perspiration beading his brows. 'These types can be dangerous,' he intoned, as we approached Bhaiyya's flat, 'murderers, thieves, it's always better to give them a wide edge.'

He didn't make love to me again. I returned to Delhi soon after, leaving Dolly bhabhi and her soon-to-be-born baby and the squalling monsoon winds.

When I returned to Delhi Suresh met me at the railway station. His stiff, awkward welcome alerted me; I too kept a guarded silence. Only the next day, at breakfast, shuffling his newspaper and wiping the yellow yolk from his face, did he broach the subject. 'I heard something, some gossip, about you and B.R.,' he said portentously. Then, almost apologetically, 'He was your ex-boss, you know, and it is very easy for people to talk.'

I feigned surprise.

'I trust you absolutely. But even then it is not good for women from good families to be talked about,' he continued heavily.

'I met him once with Paro,' I pretended to stammer. And yet in my heart, I was as sure and confident as a rock that I could handle Suresh.

He reacted instantly.

'So Paro told me, the poor girl was very upset,' he said. I breathed more freely; I had not been found out, I was safe.

'By the way, I have called Paro and a few friends for dinner,' he said, changing the subject, his suspicions quite allayed, the poor fool.

'What do you think I should cook, Suresh?' I snapped to immediate attention, the good wife who has been given a reprieve.

'I want to take them out for dinner,' he said importantly. That left me stumped. Suresh was too mean to ever take anybody out for dinner unless they rated an A+ on his contacts list. Paro, as a non-paying client, was valuable as a conversation piece at dinner-parties at home. However, I kept silent. I knew better than to go asking for trouble.

I was wary about having dinner with Paro, but to show my fear would have given me away. So I dressed with extra care, modestly, but achieving a clever mix of glamour and bhartiya nari looks – a clinging chiffon, a gold bindi, a gajra, a small gold purse.

We had a driver now. 'Paro Memsahib ke ghar,' I said peremptorily. Paro lived in a barsati at Jorbagh which she called her penthouse. Suresh remained slouched in his corner and told me to go call her, so I trudged up the three floors to her small terrace apartment. Her eyes flashed with malice and hatred at the sight of me.

'Aayah…' she called, and the thin Keralite girl who looked after her child appeared. 'Babasahib ko theek se khana dena,' she said with distant formality, then, ignoring me completely, she started climbing down, traversing three floors without so much as a backward glance at me, trailing after her. Upstairs, the boy was howling for his mama. I knew that our brief friendship was dead.

She gave Suresh a quick impulsive kiss on his cheek. 'So, love, how are you?' she asked him peppily, holding on affectionately to his hands. He smiled – no, smirked – and asked, 'Where exactly does Avinendra live, Paro?'

'Eight Willingdon Crescent,' she replied. As we sped on, I was still totally in the dark as to who Avinendra was. We arrived at a large house, with a sentry at the gate. He would not let us in, at first. 'Avinendra sahib,' she said in her usual imperious fashion. He only nodded sceptically and disappeared into the entrails of the house. He reappeared to open the front gate, and we parked the car at the end of the drive. We waited in the car until Avinendra materialised; he was that same slight youth who had been with her in Bombay.

'Driver, Sahib ke liye darwaza kholo!' Suresh shrieked, struggling gallantly with the back door from the front seat. Avinendra slid in peaceably next to Paro.

'Hi,' she said indifferently in her throaty voice. Suresh introduced me, then, after a pause, continued, 'Avinendra's father is the Minister of State for Industry.' As if my sharp little brain hadn't already plumbed his puny little machinations!

43

The same little scene repeated itself at the hotel. We encountered some friends in the lobby, and, after introducing Paro, Suresh would turn to Avinendra and say, 'His father...' again the pause, 'is the Minister for Industry!' There was achievement and self-congratulation in his voice.

Once at the dinner table, Avinendra declared that he was a Marxist. He became more and more voluble, and articulate, after every drink. Suresh, who didn't normally drink on weekdays, tried very hard to keep pace. I sipped prudishly at my pineapple juice and watched the pathetic spectacle of my husband, a grown man, a professional, chamchaing and maskalagaing a callow youth whose voice had not even cracked properly. I decided to dislike Avinendra, and decided not to show it. Nevertheless, I could not but congratulate Paro on her daring and range. A luscious young minister's son – she could certainly get them.

'These bloody five-star reactionaries,' Avinendra would harangue and Paro's eyes would narrow in a way I knew well to be wary of. His eloquence was, however, quite spellbinding, and he talked of things the others in our circle did not, or at least not with this degree of involvement. He talked of corruption, politics, and corruption. 'Now this lady...' he would say, looking at Paro with an intensity which I thought was almost manic, '... is a real individual. She has the courage of her convictions. She is not a kept woman; she is free. That is why I love her.'

Paro's eyes narrowed even more in an attempt to conceal and suppress her triumph at this declaration of love. Mockery and self-satisfaction clashed in their green depths. Then, suddenly, she switched roles. She was now the free woman, symbol and prototype of emancipation and individuality. 'I am myself,' she said theatrically, 'and no one else. I depend on nobody. I am my own person.'

For perhaps the first time in my life I got provoked. 'But, Paro,' I said logically, 'you are not your own person. You live off B.R.'s divorce settlement and by selling the jewellery he gave you. You don't – you can't – even earn your own living.'

There was a stunned silence. Suresh's anger was palpable, and so was Avinendra's agitation, but I sensed that he could not focus his anger upon me. He just looked horrified, until Paro broke the silence. 'You little bitch...' she exploded, 'I do have something you can never touch. I have my Art.'

This was the first I had even heard of her art, but I decided that enough was enough and bit my tongue to silence. 'That is not what I meant,' I said to the hostile wall of their solidarity. 'I mean...' But they all changed the subject, and nobody talked to me much for the rest of the evening.

When we returned home, Suresh was furious. For the first time in our marriage, he hit me. Again and again, angrily, relentlessly, he punched out at my face, my breasts, my thighs, and anything and everything he could lay his hands upon. 'You stupid woman,' he said, 'what were you when I married you? You were a nobody – a secretary in an office – I gave you status! What are you without me? How dare you behave like that with my friends?'

I burst into tears and sobbed loudly and piteously long into the night. The next morning I was quiet and withdrawn. Soon he began feeling sorry for me.

'I am sorry, Priya,' he said, 'I didn't mean it like that.'

As he fondled my hair in a clumsy caress, I responded with a passionate kiss, and soon enough we had made up. I was always very careful with him after that.

Avinendra had, in the meanwhile, become something of a permanent fixture in our house. He would drop in at all times of the day, and without ever being intrusive make himself helpful and companionable over whatever it was that Suresh and I were doing. He would still talk incessantly and, I thought, a little naively, about Marxism. I see now that it was only perhaps because of his extreme youth, and because he hadn't any opportunity to really harden himself against the nauseating excesses of privilege and deprivation, especially from the privileged vantage point of that ministerial bungalow. And so he used his 'Marxism' like a cheap mantra.

Suresh, too, obligingly confessed to similarly ardent views, and they would have fevered discussions late into the night, over the Scotch whisky Suresh reserved for Avinendra. (When by himself Suresh drank Indian whisky, and for the majority of his friends he preferred to serve rum or beer.) The room was always a haze of cigarette smoke and arrested alcoholic excitement when I entered, late in the night, to open the windows and clean up after them.

Suresh also managed, through effort, innuendo and application, to get on close terms with Avinendra's father's private secretary. At times, when Avinendra had gone to his hometown with his father to nurture the constituency, the private secretary would come home for dinner; he too rated a Scotch whisky. Once, Paro dropped by when the secretary was there, and Suresh was thrown into a tiny fit of consternation. But Paro took it in her stride. 'Mr Parekh,' she said to him, in an even, assured, gently wheedling tone, the sort I spent a lifetime imitating, 'you have to help me get a phone connection, please.'

'Of course, Madame,' he said abjectly, his eyes fixed lasciviously on her breasts, which were literally spilling out of her small blouse. 'Of course, Madame, mention not, you have only to mention and give me the papers.' She had the phone within a month.

One evening, after Avinendra returned, he was very worked up about 'That bloody corrupt Parekh…' I watched silently, while neither Paro nor Suresh ventured anything about Parekh – Suresh looked anxiously at me for a moment, out of the corner of his eyes, but I kept my eyes prudently downcast, the better to hide my smirk.

Paro had become an important woman, and I was wondering how to mend fences with her. The insidious web of friends, and Contacts, was coming into operation. We, too, had introduced several friends to Avinendra, who had helped them out with various little problems. These friends, in turn, helped us out in numerous little ways, and soon we had our own little house built in Greater Kailash.

What Avinendra did for a living was a mystery to me; it could have been anything. He claimed he was studying for his Ph.D. and writing a book. He was absolutely besotted by Paro, but his parents were shocked to their core by the whole affair and just couldn't believe that their Vinnie could have anything to do with 'that kind of woman'. However, their love had progressed from clandestine visits to her barsati flat to the stage where she spent most of her days, and many of her nights, at Eight Willingdon Crescent.

'That bastard,' she told me once (referring to Avinendra's father), 'is even more horny for me than Daddy was.' Daddy, of course, being Rai Bahadur, B.R.'s father. I was horrified, but suddenly she remembered her animosity and the wall rose between us again. 'Anyway, you must be knowing better,' she said, her eyes glittering with spite. Her language grew even more loose and vulgar every passing day, and even her appearance had become somehow sluttish. I had become an absolute prude in guilty reaction to my brief adulterous fling, and I winced. I wondered what Avinendra would have to say if he heard her talking like that, then concluded philosophically that he would probably love it.

She wanted to marry him, I think, because once, when I entered Suresh's chamber, I found them discussing paternity and alimony and remarriage. Paro directed her usual look of pure malice in my direction, flashed a smile at Suresh and left.

Avinendra, in the meanwhile, had become something of an ally in this dismembered quartet. He would call me Didi, and talk of ordinary things, and one Raksha Bandhan day, when I tied a Rakhi on his thin fragile wrist, he left abruptly and returned half an hour later with a beautiful Bengali cotton sari for me.

I noted with concern that he had begun to drink heavily. I also suspected that he took drugs. He seemed even one remove further from reality than at our first meeting at the rooftop restaurant.

He would sit and explain Marxism with me at great length, quite oblivious to my obvious indifference to the subject. His hero was Lenin; he even had his beard trimmed Lenin style, and though he could never sacrifice his kurtapyjama to theatrical effect, the demagogic posture, the angle of his head, the tilt of his body, in the course of his impassioned harangues, certainly bore striking resemblance to Lenin.

So, affectionately, I began to call him Lenin. He was quite pleased with the nickname. 'John or Vladimir Ilyich?' he asked. 'Both revolutionaries, in their ways, you know.'

Actually, after a while I became quite well acquainted with workaday Marxist cant, and could conduct a fairly rational and well-informed conversation on politics. The symmetry and formal perfection of the dialectical model struck some kind of chord in me. I loved it with the same fervour that I loved the clean formality of my well-ordered drawing-room.

Lenin would confide in me about Paro's increasingly irrational behaviour. He was completely dependent upon her emotionally, and I wondered sometimes whether it was a mother fixation or something psychological like that. They looked a little ludicrous in juxtaposition – Paro, massive, towering, dressed in large handloom prints and chunky jewellery, with daubs of kohl under her eyes, her frizzy hair hennaed a deep shade of red; and Lenin, in his crumpled kurta-pyjama, trailing behind her as she stormed in and out of cars, houses, lobbies, like a leaf in a summer aandhi.

One night they had a massive fight. It was past one o'clock when we heard the bell ring shrilly, accompanied by an insistent thumping on the door. Lenin was very high, and walking with the extra careful gait of someone who is trying very hard not to appear drunk. He would nevertheless teeter a little every now and then, and there was a strange manic gleam in his eyes.

'I want this female out of my life,' he said, enunciating each word deliberately and very carefully, with a heroic and almost successful attempt not to slur over the ends. Paro, in the meanwhile, was a sight to behold. Her blouse was quite ripped open from the front, and her breasts were completely naked, the nipples two compelling eyes in their blank vastness. The tatters of the blouse hung in neat lines on each side like curtains at a theatre. She was weeping copiously, and her elaborate eye makeup had run in two lines down either side of her face, in symmetry, I noticed, with the tatters of her blouse.

'See what this prick has done to me!' she shrieked, throwing her breasts open for all to see and beating on them frenziedly. 'Do you want to see my cunt as well? He thinks I'm a whore – I'll show you what a whore's cunt looks like!'

Suresh looked absolutely horrified, and I did my best to calm her down. For once she was so hysterical that she forgot even her hatred of me. 'Whore – whore – call me whore!' she sobbed, still beating at her breasts. They shook like jelly, and six fascinated eyes stayed glued to them until she curled herself up on the sofa and abandoned herself to serious sobbing. 'Is that what I left B.R. for?' she wept. 'He had his whores and wanted me to take it. But I left him and his money –' She began pulling at her hair now in her frenzy. 'To hear this baby, who I love like my son, calling me a whore? To hear this?!' Her face crumpled, and another convulsion of tears overcame her.

She was getting quite filmi now, and suddenly I was reminded of my mother. Lenin was watching in horror, and I could see that the tide of his emotions had changed, and that the magnetism of her moonlike body held him in as complete a thrall as ever before. He bent down and began feverishly to kiss her feet; she gave him a hard kick on his face, then on his groin. Then she ran out of the room, into our bedroom, and bolted the door behind her.

'Let her calm down,' Suresh said, as I started off busily towards the kitchen to get some coffee. I remember startling a sea of cockroaches in the kitchen, they seemed to be having a secret conclave. Soon we were settled quite cosily over our coffee, and the conversation too was running on normal rails. In fact Suresh was trying to edge in a word about his friend (a client from Bombay) who wanted an appointment with Lenin's father. I thought the timing was bad, but I kept silent.

As Suresh started off on a long conversation about his friend's problems, Lenin began to get a little restive. 'I must make a move now,' he said, 'let me get Paro.'

He went to the door and started knocking gently. 'Paro, love, let's go,' he said. 'Paro, maph kar do.' There was an ominous silence from within. He banged louder, and then yet louder. Then Suresh started knocking on the door as well. 'Paro! O pagal ladki!' he said. Still no reply. Suresh edged his substantial frame even closer to the door and gave it a heavy push. It opened, and the chitkan clattered like a lizard down my direct line of vision. All of us stumbled into the room together. Paro lay on the bed, quite inert. Blood dripped from her wrists to little puddles down the floor. My ladies' shaving razor lay by her side on the bed.

Her breath came faintly, and her pulse was almost imperceptible. I rushed to the bathroom and got some gauze for bandages. Then I got some sugar from the kitchen and daubed it on her bleeding wrists until she looked like a kidnapped heroine in a children's story.

When we returned from the hospital almost six hours later, it was morning. Suresh gripped me by the wrists as soon as we entered, and led me, or rather pulled me, to the bedroom. The room was a complete mess; her blood still lay all about my bed. Urgently, he locked the door. The upper latch had broken in the morning fracas, so he bent down with painful effort to fasten the small stiff latch at the bottom of the door. Then he pulled at my blouse and tore it off. He hurled me on the bed and threw himself on me.

'You whore,' he kept saying. 'You bloody whore.' We made love until I was dry and sore, but he was relentless. Just as he was climaxing, the phone began to ring in the next room. There was no one to pick it up, and it kept ringing for quite some time. When he did get to answering it, it had stopped; as I heard his heavy footfall returning, I hurriedly put on my housecoat and left that disgusting room, now forever inhabited by her ghosts.

The telephone rang again, and Suresh was there to take it. Lenin's father was on the line. Even at this moment of crisis, Suresh's face wore a look of immense importance at the mere concept of being in direct communication with the minister. 'Of course, Sir, of course,' he answered reverentially.

Then he lumbered back into the bathroom, and locked the door behind him. I could hear him humming in the shower; I sat outside, quite shattered at the prospect of having every male in my life in eternal bondage to Paro. Sighing, I got down to the more immediate task of cleaning the room.

Lenin's father had apparently requested Suresh to take over at the hospital end, so that no breath of scandal would attach to Lenin or his father over Paro's unsuccessful but dramatic suicide bid. We left for the hospital after I had hurriedly dressed under Suresh's impatient glare, his semen still crawling down my thighs. Before leaving I grabbed a book from the glass bookshelf in the drawing-room, as I had been instructed by my husband to keep Paro company through the day in her room.

I walked through the dying lawns and anaesthetised corridors of the hospital. A curtain flapped limply at the door of room number one. It was October, neither hot nor cold. She was asleep, and breathing noisily. She lay covered with a white cotton sheet, shroudlike, on the hospital bed. The pillowcase was torn, like her blouse of yesterday. Her face in sleep was heavy, solemn and grave. Her frizzy hair was beaded with sweat, and her chest rose and fell in steady rhythm.

Suresh was in a hurry to get to the court in time. A policeman appeared after about half an hour to take Paro's statement. Suresh testified that she had accidentally slashed her wrists in an attempt to open a tin of baked beans. The policeman seemed quite satisfied – he merely smirked, pirouetted, and was gone without asking any inconvenient questions whatsoever.

Lenin had sent a basket of lilies. Lilies were not, to the best of my knowledge, in season at that time, and I wondered where he had conjured them up from.

After Suresh left I was alone in tender vigil over Paro. I stared at her for some time and wondered whether she would have been able to survive a nice ordinary life. I wondered whether it was she who chased excitement or, as she claimed, the other way round. After a while

I reached for my handbag to extract the latest Mills & Boon, and was soon lost in a world of mushy romance.

Just as the heroine was abandoning her virtue Paro stirred. She yawned, her eyes fluttered open, and she looked around her.

'My God, you!' she exclaimed, all animosity forgotten in the terror and beauty of rebirth. She stretched luxuriously. 'I'm so glad I survived,' she said matter-of-factly, even complacently.

'So am I,' I replied in utter sincerity, hypnotised by so much vigour.

'I did this once before, you know,' she continued conversationally. 'It was when I was married to Bubu.' She smiled dreamily, her eyes focused on some elusive spot over my head. 'One night I returned suddenly from visiting Mummy in Delhi, to find no one at home. Bubu was in our bedroom, screwing our neighbour's daughter. I wouldn't have minded, but she saw me and began screaming, "Aunty's here! Aunty's here!"'

I listened transfixed. 'I went to the bathroom,' she continued, 'and took a Swiss army knife and scratched myself up. I hardly bled at all. When I came out of the bathroom she had already left. I showed Bubu my wounds and he laughed. It was just a little nick, he said.' She was tired, and making a soft dry sound that was neither a sob nor a laugh. 'After that, I decided I would pay him back in his own coin. I mean – every one was in love with me, and who do you think could ever love that guy?'

I could have told her, but I was getting tired of such unremitting melodrama. The edges of her vanity were showing, and the hysteria that lurked within.

Lenin entered just then, looking as slight and insubstantial as the white cotton curtain that swept in behind him, like an attendant page. It swung back, then limply re-entered the room in rhythm with the soft whirring of the ceiling fan to usher in my husband Suresh, resplendent in court regalia; his black and white pinstripe trousers hugging his portly figure, his underarms encircled with sweat, and his eyes, as ever, expressionless and slightly vacant.

'I want to go home,' I said, and left before anyone could protest or assign any more chores to me. I was beginning to lose self-control and the hospital smells were making me sick. The taxi stand was near the main entrance to the hospital. Heat and dust and disease irradiated the cityscape. Misery and filth swirled all around me, and I found strange courage and solace in the leprous beauty: every fly and mosquito, every wheezing widow and nauseous gestatory mother sang of survival. I was quite revived by the time I returned home.

I went and curled up in bed, my fingers groping for the warm secure place between my thighs. I napped lightly for a while, and then I began to masturbate. I did not fantasise, but sometimes I became Paro, and sometimes I was myself. Sometimes I was B.R. devouring Paro, and then B.R. tenderly loving Priya, and then I became Suresh who was ravishing Paro, and then Paro with Suresh in slavish possession, and intermittently Suresh copulating with Priya who was actually Paro. I was all these people; fragments of their thoughts, feelings, terrors passed through my writhing body. It was as if the basically voyeuristic nature of my life had been forever laid bare. I was possessed. The bed which lay stained with her blood and Suresh's semen was now soaked with my sweat and my lonely masquerading passion. I do not know how long I lay there; Suresh's insistent knocking barely registered, and it was a long time before I got up wearily to open the door. He entered to find me rumpled and sweaty, and the smells of spent and latent passions hung thick and heavy about the room. I do not know what primitive lusts had inhabited us, but immediately on entering the room he unzipped his trousers and took me again. This time I could not even pretend to come, and lay hot, sticky and inert under him. He grunted dissatisfiedly. Then, suddenly, I became Paro again; he sensed the heat in me, and the urgency. Our bodies ground in glorious unison, lights flashed, bells clanged, the earth moved, and we climaxed together. It was with tenderness that we arose from our nuptial bed, the darkness in the room dissolved, the ghosts dispelled.

Suresh went for a shower and emerged, smelling of baby talc, his fat body wrapped in a towel, whistling a happy filmi tune. I went to the kitchen and started organising dinner. I changed the sheets after that, getting out a new embroidered set. As we slid into bed that night, the clean soft linen caressed us, and the comforting light of the bedside lamp sang lullabies of joy and harmony. (I had brushed my hair a hundred strokes and tied it back with a pink satin ribbon.) I reached out for a book to read; Mills & Boon had never failed me before, and

Suresh's breath rose and fell in comforting rhythm.

Paro soon bounced back to normal. Her hold over Lenin had become even more vice-like after her suicide attempt, for Lenin was now riven by constant guilt and terror lest her 'death wish' overtake her again. She used her tactical advantage as only Paro could – shamelessly and relentlessly. She became an absolute tyrant. Everytime anybody disagreed with her, she had but to hint that perhaps life was no longer worth living for Suresh and Lenin to become quite distraught and rush panicked to her outrageous bidding. 'After all, she is so highly strung,' they would whisper in consternation.

I got quite sick of all this hammy melodrama. One day I asked her outright how it was that she managed to manipulate people the way she did. I mean, I always did my duty and worried about other people's feelings, and never even got a 'thank you' in return; everybody just took me even more for granted than ever before. And here she was, twisting everybody around her little finger. It was just emotional blackmail, I said.

'Oh, no!' she replied. 'It's part of being a Beautiful Woman. It's a fulltime occupation. And much harder work than it seems. But' – nodding sagely – 'it has its rewards, I confess.'

I wished I was the kind of woman who could say things like that.

But she was a faddist at heart. I remember her silly short-lived enthusiasms, which all of us were supposed to fall in with. First there were the yoga classes, which she made Lenin join along with her. She would insist that he wake up early in the morning, and drive her down to the India Gate Lawns, where, according to Lenin, they had to undergo all kinds of gruesome physical contortions in public.

Her enthusiasm was almost a primitive exhibitionism, actually. She would show off her skills to all and sundry, quite unmindful of the suitability of the occasion.

There was this chic cocktail party which an industrialist friend of Lenin's was hosting at his farm. Even Paro was quite excited about it. She dressed to the hilt, in a dull green-and-gold South Indian silk, which reflected the colour of her eyes, somehow. She wore a lot of old-fashioned jewellery as well, and flowers in her hair. It took us hours to drive to the farm, for the roads were really bumpy, and we lost our way once. But Paro was as full of beans as ever when we arrived; and determined to dazzle them all, whatever the means. And dazzle them she did.

Once she had downed a few whiskies she looked as though a bulb had been lit inside her, and a sort of electric energy field seemed to surround her. Lenin, Suresh and I hovered around her like shadows; or like moths, I thought poetically. There were a lot of moths, actually, and all kinds of other insects, as the farm was near the Yamuna river. The atmosphere was quite tranquil, even a little subdued, in spite of all the pretty fairy lights and soft Shehnai music. It was, I could see, going to be a very proper party.

Suresh determinedly set about circulating. When we met, half an hour later, Paro was deep in conversation with a very handsome man. Suresh told me, very importantly and a shade too loudly, that he was a Rich and Famous industrialist, who owned textile mills, and oil mills, and God knows what else. 'Rich and Handsome' I thought wistfully. His wife – or girlfriend, or whoever it was that he was with – was a very beautiful woman as well. She was wearing a stunning sheer net sari with a daring little blouse. I felt cold even looking at her, and pulled my pashmina shawl tightly around me.

I could see that Paro was bent on conquest. Her lips were parted, her eyes narrowed, and the speculative look I knew so well was rising in her eyes. The woman in the net sari began wilting; her smile froze as she observed Paro's untimid advances. It remained frozen for some time, and was then transmuted into a sort of tremulous threatening snarl.

I could not hear what Paro was saying. But the man seemed intrigued; he looked appeasingly at his date first, and then seemed to forget her presence completely.

Suddenly I found Paro throwing down her pallav and wrapping it around her waist, lungi style, and before I could even figure out what was happening, she was on the grass, sandals kicked off, and two long beautiful white legs pointing like cranes to the night sky. She stood like that, on her head, for over a minute, in perfect confident balance; the eyes of every single person at the party were riveted to those long alabaster legs. She looked so . . . nude, somehow. Her legs were really white and perfectly shaped, and I could even glimpse her shadowed thighs and black lace panties.

Lenin and Suresh rushed up to her to form a sort of protective cordon. But she was on her feet again, flushed, triumphant, not at all embarrassed. 'We were just talking about yoga,' she said nonchalantly, before they encircled her and led her sternly home. We left a trail of shocked unbelieving looks and incredulous whispers behind us.

And then, there were her salad days. I still remember how all of us had to suffer her new-found passion for greens and things uncooked. 'Cooking is unhealthy, unnatural, and unhygienic,' she would declare with all the fervour of a convert. She called us over for a Sunday Salad Lunch once. She had also invited a friend of Lenin's, a young man called Arif who worked for the B.B.C. in London, and who consequently spoke only the chastest Urdu in ethnic self-defence. We basked in the beatific Delhi sunshine, listening to his tall stories, slugging down gin after gin.

But Maryamma, Paro's Keralite ayah, had fallen ill just that morning. 'Oh, Priya and I will handle the kitchen while you boys have fun,' she said airily. Then led me to the kitchen, demonstratively friendly for once. There were loads of vegetables stuffed inside a stinking shopping bag. 'Just wash these,' she said, 'while I fix Arif a drink.' She popped in again just as I had finished washing the lettuce, carrots and spring onions, put the beetroot to boil, and shelled the peas; I was warily examining the bruised mushrooms when she came to inspect my labours. 'Do you know how to cut radishes into scallops?' she asked hopefully. I confessed I did not, and she skipped out again. She didn't return for hours, and when I went in search of her, Arif was spouting extravagant Urdu shairi about her being like a zephyr, a spring breeze, a monsoon shower and things like that. I settled down to listen, but she quickly shooed me back into the kitchen. 'I think you haven't sliced the cucumbers evenly,' she said remonstratively, and yet with a touching woebegone air. She munched at a carrot or two while I got out the plates and napkins.

'Oh, Priya, what about the aesthetics,' she exclaimed despairingly as she came to review my final handiwork. 'I don't think the red of these squashy tomatoes goes with the colour of the carrots.' Then she got out a packet of imported cheese from somewhere and cut it into squiggledy little squares and threw it over everything, and announced enthusiastically to everybody that lunch was ready.

Of course nobody dared be anything but extravagantly taken with the lunch. I choked on every morsel. 'Priya cooked everything, really,' Lenin ventured loyally, and got a dirty look from Paro for that.

Naturally, Suresh was famished by the time we got home. 'That was a rather inadequate lunch, Priya,' he said chidingly.

I almost threw a tantrum. 'I thought your Paro was too good at everything,' I said spitefully.

'But you know she's not meant for the kitchen,' he said indulgently, a dreamy light entering his eyes, 'and besides it was you who made the lunch.'

I fried him pakodas for tea-time, and he gorged himself disgracefully.

Those were happy days for all of us. My happiness assumed a special shape, for, after all these years, I found myself pregnant at last. When the lady doctor confirmed the good news, Suresh was deliriously happy – so much so that it really jolted me and made me wonder how much he must have felt the absence of a child all these years.

It was ironical, I reflected a little bitterly, that even my child was probably conceived, after so many years of sterility, at a moment when I was, in my subconscious, pretending to be Paro. I knew, with an unshakable certainty, that it had happened 'that night', the night when she had tried to kill herself. I did my best to keep away from her, for I knew her knack for destroying anything that resembled an innocent happiness. My middle-aged body had difficulty in responding to another life within it. I would be violently sick in the mornings. I grew to a grotesque size. Yet my life assumed meaning and purpose; distant relatives wrote to me again. (Suresh had broadcast the good news to everyone possible.) Bhaiya offered to send Dolly bhabhi to look after me. I knitted sweaters, and shawls and booties for my unborn child – I embroidered bedsheets and pillowcases and stitched nappies and searched for a suitable ayah.

We planned together for our son (though I hoped, secretly, for a daughter). My face grew softer, and I gave money to beggars. Suresh looked after me with tender care.

I told nobody that I was terrified of the thought and act of childbirth. I had heard so much about the pain of parturition that I would awaken screaming soundlessly in the dead of the night, my body covered with cold sweat. The doctor reassured me that it was only gas, but I knew better. It was terror.

I even developed blood pressure. Everywhere I was followed by the genii of Suresh's solicitude. Suddenly, our life attained mutuality. After all, I was carrying our child, whom we would bring up and who would inherit our goods, and look after us in our old age. Suresh was an only child and it struck me that he was in fact a very lonely man.

We had been so wrapped up in my pregnancy that we had become quite anti-social. Suresh's birthday was approaching, and I decided to give a small dinner party. Just a few friends, a few lawyer couples, and of course, Paro and Lenin. I wanted to avoid them, for in my delicate condition I had no stomach for melodrama, but there was no way I could really do so. I got to work lovingly on the dinner, planning the menu, shopping myself for fresh vegetables and meat, and so on. I had a nasty moment at the I.N.A. market, when a cow walked into me and almost gored me with its horns. Panicked, I hid behind a car, my heart panting wildly. When I told Suresh, he was really disturbed and forbade me to leave the house alone.

I had prepared an elaborate combination of Indian and continental food for dinner. I had also arranged flowers all about the hall, and everything looked festive and happy. There were about a dozen people for dinner. I had taken special pains to dress well, and even went to the hairdresser to have my hair done. She made me an elegant low bun, and I pinned a yellow rose to it to match my yellow silk sari.

Everyone was happy and decorous and well behaved; everyone drank in moderation, and the party broke up early, in deference to my delicate condition. Paro came alone, as Lenin was out of town. She was looking beautiful and well groomed, and she was surprisingly low key all evening.

Later, as I was tidying up after all the guests had left, Suresh held me by the wrists and stopped me. 'Please, Priya, for my son's sake, if not your own,' he said pleadingly. I rather liked all this attention, and settled down cosily on the sofa with my feet up.

'Let's open your presents,' I said contentedly, and we sat like two children amidst the cards and ribbons and wrapping paper. The Johoreys had got Suresh a leather desk-diary, and a client, also an old friend, had got him a Gold Cross ballpen. Then there was a Lucknowi kurta, and some books, and yet more flowers.

Paro's huge rectangular gift was wrapped in sheets and sheets of newspapers and brown paper. Finally we unearthed an oblong etching, in metal and bronze, of a screaming woman. There was a staring totemic sort of owl in the foreground, and the woman's eyes were round and glazed with terror. Her hair streamed and flew about her face in furious swirls. Suresh stared at it for some time. 'Modern Art,' he said finally, 'you'd better put it in the guest bedroom.'

I was speechless. 'It is horrible,' I said. I wondered if Paro had smelled out my fears, or whether she thought we might like the screaming face.

That night it happened. I lost my baby. Never before, and never after, have I known such pain. I am referring not to the physical pain, which was negligible, but to the desolation, the sudden emptying out of reason and beauty and hope from life. In fact, even today, I can hardly bear even to write about it. The sheets of our sturdy double bed were stained red with murderous congealed blood; I went in a rickety ambulance, dark as the night, to the noisy nursing home, where the bored doctor on duty aborted me.

As I lay anaesthetised in my iron hospital bed, I could hear someone droning on in the next room, 'The whole trouble with India is that people who can, have no children... and so these bloody muslims and harijans...'

And so life returned to normal, a little emptier, more brittle, but otherwise much as before. Suresh was very nice to me. But I could see that the hurt ran deep, and he threw himself into his work with a vengeance. Soon, he was almost in the top bracket in his profession in Delhi. Of course, he got busier and busier, and I saw even less of him than before.

For a long time I carried the stigmata of my guilt, for I was certain that fate had smelled out my fears and killed my child. In my dreams I was a plastic flowerpot covered with white pebbles. I even saw a psychiatrist, but he said nothing, and I felt uncomfortable discussing sex and things with him; besides, he charged sinful fees. So I stopped the consultations and was soon normal again. I joined a group of friends at their kitty parties, and made many new acquaintances. The trouble with India, according to most of them, was that servants were going from bad to worse, and the more one did for them the more ungrateful they were.

Time healed my wounds; the first flush of unhappiness soon subsided. I redecorated the house, and I changed my hairstyle.

Lenin's father was no longer a minister – he fell out of favour, and was reshuffled. And then, in the by-election, he didn't even get a renomination. Lenin shifted into Paro's barsati, for he just couldn't bring himself to return to his home town in Madhya Pradesh. Things were going downhill for him. He was still working on his doctoral thesis on the dynamics of class relationships; he was balding at an alarming rate, and looked too old to be a student any more. He and Paro would sit on the baked brick floor of their terrace, the heat rising around them in little steamy clouds, parched earth all around them, and empty broken flowerpots, withered skeletons of hibiscus and night flowers. They were always careless and would forget to water the plants – and in any case there was a constant water shortage on the third floor. Sometimes they would empty their gin glasses into the parched gamlas – once I even saw a very drunk Lenin stagger towards a flowerpot and urinate unevenly over it. But even that couldn't help those poor plants survive. And yet small saplings of peepal, and mango, grew untended on the cracks between the terrace wall, and sprouted clean fresh leaves even through those hostile summers and still monsoons.

Paro was a child of privilege. I couldn't remember her ever passionately wanting anything; she took the luxury and adulation that surrounded her for granted, as part of the perks. But now, with a despondent Lenin by her side, she had her first experience of deprivation, of the indignities of need. She didn't know about queues, and rationcards, and bus-routes; and I don't think she even tried to learn; she only shut out that world, slugging down gin after gin and surviving in stubborn hope.

I could see that Suresh wanted desperately to drop Lenin and Paro, for they had become something of a social embarrassment. Paro had grown huge and obese, and hennaed her hair to a deep unnatural red. Her eyes and nails and other extremities screamed with outrageous, discordant, colour-schemes of pinks and golds, greens and mauves, blues and maroons. Once she even painted her fingernails in gold and red stripes. She took to flaunting the most astoundingly low necklines, and all eyes would stand riveted to those careless displays of mammary volume. I sensed that she needed to display the remnants of her sexuality amidst the obese wreck of her body – it was like a flagship in a war-devastated land. I wondered whether she and Lenin were on drugs; I watched, amazed at their sudden slide into social degradation. The process was so abrupt, so compelling, that it left no time for obfuscation – they were social debris, and there were no excuses either for them or for us.

Lenin's mind had brief flares of lucidity, even brilliance. He still insisted that he was a student, and clung desperately to the formlessness and anarchy of youth. He still smoked Charminars, and carried his tattered jhola with its load of dog-eared radical Penguins. He seemed imprisoned in a time bubble; his friends all seemed to have settled down to careers and wives, and many had already graduated to their first divorce. His insistence on his youth was pathetic, a conscious rejection of responsibility and adulthood. The departure of his father, of whom he had always been terrified, had a curious dual effect, for Lenin was both prodded to a sort of growth and yet inhibited by precharted parental lifeplans. He glimpsed distant horizons and yet fled from all possible shores of immediate anchorage. He clung to Paro with absolute and unyielding need, in fact he unconditionally worshipped her. And she too, in turn, perhaps survived only because of his need.

And yet they hated each other and would bicker constantly, and my practised feminine eye observed that Paro was on the lookout for a saviour to get her out of this mess. And then, one day, the unthinkable happened. Lenin won a lottery. At first we thought it was some kind of a joke. The familiar insistent ringing at the doorbell in the middle of the night, and both of them, in apparent harmony, and slightly inebriated as usual. He held a bunch of multi-coloured gas balloons in his hand, and they fluttered over his head like a benediction.

'Deus Ex Machina,' Lenin announced sonorously, and extracted a bottle of champagne from under his shawl. We had a copy of Latin for Lawyers in Suresh's library but so much erudition and class went right over my head. 'Saved by the bell,' he clarified.

'He's won a fucking lottery,' Paro amplified. She was dressed in a long black kaftan, and her hair lay loose about her shoulders, the red highlights giving her an eerie flamboyance. I sensed that she was not being flippant, for there was a subtle change in her demeanour, and her arrogance, which had appeared a little threatened recently, seemed to have resurfaced without any major bruises. Her contempt for me was once again visible and tangible.

I never knew such things happened in real life. I thought such things happened only in films. In fact it had all begun with a film. One drunken night Lenin and Paro decided to 'go slumming' and see a Bachhan starrer. One of Amitabh's dialogues really appealed to Lenin.

'Apna naseeb kabhi kisi ko mat becho,' Amitabh Bachhan had said, and that was what Lenin was now repeating in excellent declamatory style, his eyebrows all askew. He told us the whole involuted story of the film, the upshot being that he (Lenin), went and bought himself a lottery ticket. He didn't forget about it after that, but kept the ticket (for Lenin) very carefully, and assiduously checked all the results in the newspapers on the due date. He swore that he was not in the least surprised to find that he had won five lakhs of rupees.

'I always knew that something would – you know – happen,' he said, his eyes vacant with relief. 'It was sort of… pre-ordained you know. I mean, God looks after his own.'

'And the devil,' Paro said complacently, as Suresh fiddled with the champagne bottle.

I must say that I was very impressed; things like this could happen only to Paro and those in her daemonic charmed circle.

Suresh was trying to remodulate his voice to suit the occasion; I could read his mind like a Dhobi account book, for he really was becoming more and more obvious with every passing day. With the lottery as a crutch, Lenin might well be on his way to social recovery. 'You must be very careful now, yaar,' he said solicitously. 'Get an agency or something. Fixed deposits… hmmm… I don't really know what the exact interest rates going are… and I don't know to what degree lottery winnings are taxable …' But he had already lost their interest. They were like two children, living entirely in the moment. Lenin had let go of the gas balloons and they were floating forlornly around the ceiling. I thought spitefully of Paro's child, as lost and without moorings as the playthings of these juvenile and inebriated delinquents.

We finished the champagne, toasting fate, and luck, and destiny. Then we graduated to whisky. They left after consuming every drop of Scotch that we had in stock. We had decided to meet for lunch the next day.

'Five lakhs,' Suresh said, tossing and weighing the figure before abandoning himself to fitful sleep. I could see him calculating, forwards, backwards, and sideways, at the exact value of the sum, in terms of cases, air fares, property prices, and every other conceivable means of exchange.

★

They spent almost a lakh just on redecorating their

barsati flat. They gave a little party, a 'second house warming', for their friends. Suresh was horrified at the extravagance. 'It's not even their own house,' he kept muttering to himself, for Lenin and Paro were too full of the future to even listen. The two-bedroom flat had been painted entirely black – black walls, black roof, and black wall-to-wall carpeting. There were mirrors on the ceiling. I suppose it was very chic really. Paro had persuaded the landlord to let her convert the terrace into a rooftop lawn. There was even a little swing in the corner. (Paro, Lenin and her school-going son were all rumoured to share the same bedroom, for which Paro had bought black satin bedsheets.)

On the night of the party, the black sky, the green-black lawn, the green-and-black interior of the flat, Paro herself dressed in a dark gown (a gown, not a kaftan) that looked like something Imelda Marcos might wear, with pleated butterfly sleeves. Green eyeshadow flecked her face under heavily pencilled brows; she looked like an alien, an encounter from a sci-fi film.

The crowd was a carefully orchestrated mix of the right people. The mandatory politician, artist, businessman were all there. There were a few surprise items, such as, for example, Lenin's sister, who was married to an I.A.S. officer and in Delhi for a visit. I wondered if she was The Family, or the Middle Class Intellectual Elite. She seemed utterly disoriented in those strange surroundings, and we formed a natural bond. In fact, I found I could even play the sophisticate to her, without any visible strain on credibility.

The food was, of course, terrible. There was a flat, warm and insipid white wine, and soggy canapés on monaco biscuits; putrid biryani, from the backlanes of Jama Masjid, and rasmalai from the local sweet shop.

But of course everyone was too drunk to care, and enjoying themselves hugely. Paro was very relaxed and buoyant – she was laughing her deep belly laugh, and cracking loud vulgar jokes. I could feel all my buried insecurities resurfacing. Fifteen years to the day since I had first met her, I was now the more socially secure/respectable/established, and yet here I was, feeling as gauche as ever inside, sitting in a corner and discussing the servant problem with Lenin's sister from Jabalpur.

The party was really getting out of control – everybody was slightly high, and the patent unreality of the situation (uski to lottery nikal gayee, they would giggle) was infectious. Paro's smuggler friend, who, it was whispered, was the cocaine king of Delhi, was getting into a heated argument about Nehru with some young intellectuals, Nehru having found an incongruous but fervent supporter in this rabid balding and very profane man. Suresh was busy toadying up to some government officials, and a bearded barefoot artist was busy making charcoal sketches of Paro, most unflattering ones, which however she seemed quite delighted with. The Government official's wife was getting exasperated by the general pandemonium and nagging him to go home. It was quite a circus, in short.

Suddenly, something electric seemed to grip the air. Paro was breathing a little harder than usual, and her nostrils were slightly distended, like a mare's. Her demeanour betrayed the slightest hint of tension, of withholding. It was almost as if she were sniffing unfamiliar territory. Staring at her across the room was the ugliest, grossest and vilest man I had ever seen. He was black as the night, black as the carpet, and his belly protruded obscenely from his chest, like a fat rotting pear. All this was balanced on the thinnest, spindliest legs possible. An immaculately starched white khadi topi nestled on his thick, suspiciously black hair. He was dressed in a starched white Khaddar kurta with a jacket, below which he wore an almost transparent dhoti. He was swirling – yes, swirling – an ivory topped cane. He looked at her directly, with undisguisedly speculative sexual interest, and for perhaps the first time in my life I saw Paro blush. Slowly a deep scarlet colour travelled down her face towards those flagrant breasts; but of course her superb social self-control took over.

'I am Paro, and this is my party. And who may you be?' she asked him in chaste hindustani (as against her Memsahib hindi reserved for servants and panwallahs). She was direct, even curt, and by now not in the least embarrassed. Paro could really be very rude when she wanted to be.

'My party is the Congress party – and I have come here to see Avinendra, to congratulate him upon his good fortune – upon his many good fortunes,' he leered, not in the least put out. 'Myself Shambhu Nath Mishra – you might have seen my name in papers sometimes.'

The enigma of the disproportionate power emanating

from this strange personality suddenly cleared. Shambhu Nath Mishra was one of the most controversial politicians of the day, an eminence grise, a sinister minister.

For the rest of the evening, he and Paro were inseparable. They sat in a corner of the terrace, near the swing, absolutely oblivious to the rest of the people at the party, to the high-pitched laughter and to the dinner lying cold on the buffet tables. Lenin was getting more and more agitated – in fact the poor boy was almost in tears. Every few minutes he would go to call her in for dinner, or whisper something in her ear, probably begging her to come in and join the rest of the party, but she would impatiently wave him away. Mishra was holding her hand and slyly stroking it; she was responding feverishly, obscenely, like a cat in heat.

After a while she rose to leave with him. Lenin said, in an absolutely desolate and pathetic voice, 'Paro, please not just now, please.'

'Don't be silly. Just look after Junior and see that he has his dinner. I'll just have a paan and return,' she said imperiously. I suddenly remembered the existence of that withdrawn and retiring child, and wondered in which corner of the crowded house he was hiding. His timid frail body looked very much like Lenin's – in fact there seemed to be a bond of shared and mutual need between them.

She left in an almost mesmeric trance, and returned more than an hour later with the strangest expression on her face. It was exaltation and bondage, a hypnotic, almost hysterical contentment. Paan stains darkened her mouth, looking most incongruous with the chic evening dress. She had tied a gajra to her hair, and another to her wrist. Mishra, too, was disdainfully sniffing at a fragrant white circlet of night-flowers; she looked fucked, used, what Suresh would have called a G.B. road type. An unease, a pall, descended on the party, as if everyone sensed that something strange was happening. Five minutes after they returned, the entire circus had disbanded.

Her affair with Mishra became one of the hottest scandals of the year. She rose swiftly and surely in social prominence, a sort of hetaira, a madonna of the garbage heaps. The lowlier papers, and hindi magazines like *Maya* and *Manohar*, delighted in lampooning her. Delhi's tawdry social circuits, too, got more than their share of C.T.'s out of the whole affair, and dinner parties were agog with malicious innuendo and speculation. But she was unconcerned and totally and absolutely enslaved.

The whole thing puzzled me. I could not understand the situation. I could well ascribe the worst possible motives to her, and suspect her of having a liaison with such an influential figure for all the implicit and unsubtle gains she could derive from her position as his mistress. What left me totally stunned was her absolute and unconditional emotional surrender.

She would stare at him in moony adoration. She would telephone him incessantly, trying always to dodge the phalanx of secretaries and officials surrounding him, trying constantly only to be with him. He would come to her barsati, and they would conveniently send Lenin away, to take Junior for an ice cream or on any such obvious excuse.

There was more than just sexuality at play here. There were the elements of fascism, of a sado-masochistic psychodrama, being enacted. Lenin and Junior watched horrified, like children at a massacre, helpless, immobilised, and secretly fascinated. Suresh was quite pleased, at first, at the prospect of another such immediate and important contact. But he soon realised, to his consternation, that she was too infatuated to even think of immediate and practical tactical gains.

One day, Suresh managed to persuade Mishraji to come for dinner. Paro was, of course, invited; there was much debate about whether or not to invite Lenin. I was adamant that Lenin come, for I wanted an ally, and besides, I was curious. Dinner was, naturally, at home, for it would not have been discreet to go to a restaurant. I spent hours slaving at the kitchen, personally supervising the most elaborate moghlai meal I could conceive. Then I got busy dusting and cleaning the house. I bought some gladioli from the florist and did some nice ikebana arrangements.

Suresh was sitting in his library when they came, together, in his car. 'Lenin is helping Junior with his homework,' she told me. At first, the evening was a stiff, sullen, silent affair. However, with a steady and dedicated consumption of alcohol (the best Premium Scotch, naturally, with some imported wines as standby) everyone soon felt quite convivial.

Everyone, that is, except me, for I was too busy fluttering around the kitchen, a glass of gin in my hand. In fact, Paro got quite drunk. Every time I enquired if I could serve dinner, she would insist, 'Not yet yaar. . .' I served endless rounds of papads, pakodas, moongphali. Finally, at midnight, I insisted that it was really time we served dinner. 'No yaar,' she insisted again, 'what's the hurry?'

Mishraji had been looking quite preoccupied. Suddenly he got up, wavering for a moment on those spindly legs. 'I must go, I have early important meeting tomorrow,' he said, with an air of weary finality.

Suresh got very upset. 'But sir, but sir. . .' he spluttered.

Paro got quite hysterical. 'Please-please-please darling, let me come with you,' she insisted. 'Let's go to Jorbagh...'

He was blunt, even dismissive. 'Do not be nuisance,' he said simply, and made his exit, twirling his cane as he left.

The three of us sat in confused silence over our dinner. Suresh, of course, still managed to polish off a large meal, but Paro was close to tears, and wouldn't eat anything. When I returned from the kitchen with the kheer (which had silver leaf on it) I caught Suresh kissing Paro passionately on her tear-stained cheeks, presumably in an effort to cheer her up. He leapt away guiltily when he saw me enter the room. She sat listlessly, absolutely unconcerned and unresponsive, almost as if he hadn't even touched her.

I was, by now, a mature woman, and knew how to handle difficult situations tactfully. Besides, Paro was looking so pathetic that I really could not bring myself to feel jealous. There was only the faintest chill in my voice as I asked them if they were ready for the kheer. But Suresh seemed really concerned for Paro, he was now holding on feverishly to her white and scarlet hands and caressing them tenderly with his own hairy, stubby paws. 'Why get so worked up over that old fart?' he asked finally in idiomatic Panjabi.

Paro's reply was devastatingly honest. 'He is so ugly, so repulsive, that he makes me feel beautiful,' she said. '…and he has something…' She became incoherent and slightly maudlin, and poured herself yet another drink.

It wasn't long before Mishraji began tiring of such smothering devotion. But the more he rejected her, the more she would thrust herself at him. It was the most pitiable spectacle of perversity and self-flagellation possible. She was utterly miserable, and so was young Junior, who no one ever called by his proper name, Aniruddha, and whom no one even noticed these days. The only person Junior could share his misery with was Lenin for, over the years, Junior had come to accept Lenin as a familiar part of the landscape. Lenin was of course the most miserable. He was fast running through what remained of his lottery money, buying extravagant presents for Paro, jewellery, shawls, anything that might catch her fancy and keep her mind and body off Mishra for a while.

He was becoming more and more withdrawn, but I think the enforced weaning was doing him good, for he was also becoming a little more positive and self-assured in the face of her subjugation and misery. He was kind to her, and tended her with the pity and love some extend to a sick animal – and Paro was indeed a love-sick animal if I ever saw one.

One morning, Mrs Shambhu Nath Mishra descended upon their barsati flat. She asked for Paro; and – according to their maid, who told our driver, who in turn, with a little prodding, disgorged the story to me – pounced upon her, literally and physically, telling her to leave her husband alone. 'Arre, teri jaisi rundi bahut dekhin hai, aati jaati,' she said.

Paro tried to be dignified and articulate, which must have been difficult in the circumstances. 'We are friends, we share a lot in common,' she replied in English.

'Yes, common – you are common type of woman,' Mrs Shambhu Nath Mishra was reported to have screamed.

'Get out, you illiterate woman,' a provoked Paro replied.

'You get out of his life, you pest,' Mrs Mishra shrieked.

Then, according to reliable channels, she found her way to the kitchen, found the jhaddoo, and smacked Paro with it across her face, leaving long red scratches across her cheeks. She then began attacking her randomly, on her body, her back, her hair, until her passion was spent.

She then exited with considerable dignity, followed by her security man, who had been waiting decorously outside the door the while. 'The trouble with India,' she was heard muttering as she left, her short dark frame shaking with rage, was that 'Desh me bas ab Rundi Raj chalta hai.'

Soon the story was all over the cocktail circuit, and Paro was once more the butt of various suggestive, sniggering jokes. They were mockingly referred to as 'Paro and Devdas', and viciousness and malice and social slights pursued Paro everywhere, cloaked of course in dinner invitations and deep concern. Still Paro remained in strange and terrible thrall. Her vivacity had quite disappeared, and she had begun to look subtly different. Shambhu Nath Mishra concealed neither his fascination nor his contempt for her. She seemed quite content, indeed happy, to be treated like a common whore.

Then summer came, and Shambhu Nath Mishra was to go to America for a World Conference on something or the other. Paro cajoled and hustled the money out of Lenin and Suresh to buy herself a ticket as well, for she was determined to accompany him. They left on the same flight, together, and she had even managed to get her ticket upgraded to first class. I don't know what happened there in the three weeks that she spent with him, but she returned alone. He was returning via Hawaii, where his daughter was settled, and he didn't want Paro to embarrass him by her presence.

She returned looking thinner, and younger, and very sexy; she had styled her hair differently, and was wearing jeans, and white khadi kurtas, which she had borrowed from Mishraji.

I had never been abroad in my life, and Paro's trip became a stormy point of recrimination between me and Suresh, for, of course, she never returned the money she had borrowed. To add insult to injury, she did not even bother to get me any of the perfumes and cosmetics I had requested in my shopping list. She bought, of all things, a huge teddy bear for Suresh; I don't know if she was trying to be funny, or what the joke was.

Lenin had been playing the surrogate father to Aniruddha during Paro's little jaunt to the States. Junior was now a tall, nervous boy with protruding ears and prominent teeth, reportedly very good in his studies. Some legal problems and disputes about custody of the poor child seemed to have surfaced. 'Bucky' Bhandpur, forgotten ghost from the past, wanted to send him to Doon for his further education. Paro was surprisingly mature about the whole thing. As I rifled through Suresh's drawers in the course of one of my routine checks on his life, I came across some papers which indicated an amicable and sensible settlement between the two.

In fact, her relationship with 'Bucky' Bhandpur seemed to have stabilised into something approaching friendship. Often, all five of us would go out for dinner together. Lenin had by now been accorded a sort of elder son status, and 'Bucky' and Paro seemed friendlier now than ever before; much friendlier, indeed, than on that night, many years ago now, when I had first met them at the Tabela and he had crashed his car on the way home.

Paro had been seeing less and less of Shambhu Nath Mishra lately; he had become like a fading echo in our lives. She rarely mentioned him, and they seemed to be living in different orbits. She appeared to have got him out of her system, and would mockingly refer to him as 'that Kala Kutta', or, more affectionately, 'Kala Bhooth', or the more esoteric 'Yamadoota'. This morbid humour apart, she really seemed to be moving towards some kind of internal stability again. I am sure that Bhandpur's undemanding friendship also helped considerably in this healing process.

So there we were, the five of us, quite companionable again, at the Café Chinois one evening, Suresh sipping his coffee like a bellows, Bucky and Paro devouring large cognacs, and Lenin spooning in mouthfuls of cassata ice cream in between large gulps of whisky. Lenin had been baiting Bucky all evening, but Bucky had consistently refused to respond to any provocation.

Lenin was being elegantly withering, in a very erudite fashion, about the re-emergence of the feudal classes in modern India. 'The trouble with India, as I am sure you will agree,' he would stammer condescendingly, 'is that as a breed you types are all half-Anglicised, and half-denationalised. And completely irrelevant, if not treacherous, to any advanced society we may dream about or plan for. In fact, I think all of you should be shot dead!'

'I say, old boy, isn't that carrying it a little too far?' Bhandpur replied abstractedly, as one might to a pesky schoolboy. This infuriated Lenin even more, and he began addressing Bucky as 'Your Excellency', or 'Your Royal Highness', or 'Maharajkumar Sahib'. On his way to the toilet he even executed a low courtesy bow to Bhandpur, and reserved an even more elaborate 'Farshi Salaam' for Paro. She seemed as tickled as a teenager at the idea of playing them off against each other, and tried subtly to push Bucky into a more aggressive stance. But he was far too seasoned a player to rise to such obvious bait.

After returning from the toilet, Lenin settled down quite peacefully to his ice cream. When he had finished, he dropped a bombshell. 'I am getting married,' he said casually. At first nobody noticed – he had regressed so completely into a state of para-adolescence that no one took him very seriously any more. He didn't repeat the statement, but lapsed into a moody silence. I heard what he said but it sort of ricocheted over my head. Lenin had grown away from me, and although I still tied a Rakhi to him whenever I could, many years he would simply forget, and he never got me a sari again.

As the silence got more and more gloomy, Bucky snapped his fingers to catch the waiter's attention. Something snapped in Lenin's mind as well; suddenly, he was on his feet, foaming at the beard.

'Bloody feudalists,' he screamed. 'Reactionaries, bloodsuckers! Can't you talk to them like human beings instead of snapping your fingers like a… they slog and slave all day and you can't spare a polite word?' He was getting more and more worked up. 'It's blood money that's paying for this dinner.' He spat the words out. 'You're eating the sweat and blood and toil of the masses, you contemptible creature. You must have been born in a harem, and brought up by slaves – feudal lobby – you were animals – you are animals.' Lenin's father's parliamentary seat, we must bear in mind, had gone to the local Maharaja type.

Bucky, too, had imbibed a considerable amount of alcohol, and was doing his best to exercise self-control.

He was half sitting, half standing – like a restless, rearing stallion, I thought to myself – like a Mills & Boon hero.

He rose, and swaying slightly, raised his glass in a sort of toast. 'I could well say, sir, that you Brahmins... a worthy race, and you jumped-up Ha'penny Tu'penny politicians,' he said with exceeding politeness, 'and their Ha'penny Tu'penny sons have tried your best to rule from behind the throne, to obscure knowledge and religion, while pretending to protect it, while all you are really protecting are your privileges. I have seen a lot of Brahmins in Bhandpur...'

Paro watched amusedly, her eyes narrowing.

'Did you say you were getting married, Lenin?' I asked, panicking at the idea of a scene and clutching at any straw I could.

'Of course I'm getting married,' he replied indignantly. 'I am marrying a sane normal reasonable girl from a sane normal respectable family and getting out of this obscene mess.'

Paro's smile shattered for a fraction of a second, her lips trembled and a sort of uncertainty descended on her face. But she quickly pulled herself together and gave out a long excited screech of joy and excitement. She planted a huge kiss on Lenin's cheeks, leaving behind a moist red imprint. 'Darling!' she exclaimed, quite without malice, 'Why didn't you tell Mummy first!' Now tears were running down her cheeks like monsoon streams, Bhandpur ordered champagne, and there was a general air of excitement and jubilation. In fact, a sort of relief filtered on to Paro's face. Lenin was a little bewildered. I think he had wanted to wound her by his engagement, and was in turn a little wounded by her apparent indifference and almost transparent relief.

Upon further prodding Lenin even produced a photograph of his fiancée – a full-length portrait of a tall slim girl with an intelligent, slightly obstinate expression. She was the daughter of a former chief minister, and her family and Lenin's had known each other very well for many years. We gathered that her father was willing to settle for a dreg like Lenin because of some astral imbalances in her horoscope – an early death was predicted for any possible future husband. Lenin, of course, dismissed such 'obscurantist superstitions', while admitting that there was something to be said after all for tradition, and caste, and a conventional marriage.

Good riddence, I thought to myself affectionately, for I was quite excited at the prospect of his wedding. But that was not all, for his future father-in-law was even willing to foot the bill for a two-year course in a prestigious foreign university for some post-doctoral ruminations. And there would, of course, be other forms of recompense, i.e. a substantial dowry probably awaited him.

His family was naturally thrilled at the prospect of their beloved Vinnie finally settling down. A fairytale ending, really, a most convenient ending to a high-spirited and carefree youth.

Paro displayed her usual sangfroid and took this new development in her stride. She immediately deployed the entire focus of her available charm at a hapless Lenin, and tried her best to reassert her old awful sway over him. She smiled winsomely, tickled his bearded chin, kickicooed him like a baby – but he seemed unflattered and totally impervious to her charms. He seemed, in fact, already to belong to another generation.

'You must help me, didi, in doing some shopping,' he said to me, stoically ignoring her coquetry. Paro threw me a look of pure venom.

'I'll do it for you, love,' she said throatily, and began getting even more overtly sexual in her blandishments. Soon, his facade of studied indifference began crumbling; for it had been just that, a tantrum to get Paro's undivided attention. They left together soon after, and we had to drop Bucky Bhandpur home, for Paro had taken his car.

He was feeling very talkative, and was apparently not at all concerned by Paro's desertion. 'You know,' he said ruminatively, 'the woman is simply extraordinary. When I first met her, eleven years ago, she was one of the silliest, sweetest girls around. Would you believe that I was her first lover?'

I felt like correcting him, but kept my silence.

'And that bugger certainly wasn't depriving himself of the good things of life,' he continued. 'He would lay anything that moved.'

His eyes turned dreamy and reminiscent. 'One day I met her at a party – my God, it really was a long time ago… she was wearing a weird silver net outfit, and trying to look very bright and peppy, and to ignore the fact that her husband was making out with a lot of the chicks around. I was nice to her, in a friendly way, and she sort of attached herself to me like a drowning person. I mean, she literally wouldn't let go of me, and any man – I mean, we started seeing a lot of each other and had what I suppose you would call an affair. Soon this sewing machine magnate – what's his name, her dear husband, found out that she just wasn't spending her afternoons sitting at home with her sewing machines any more.

'And he threw her out, literally, he and that rabid father of his, and I was left holding the pieces. It was a dashed funny situation – I mean, it was just a harmless fling, but no go. But I was in a real quandry, for I was, you know, sort of engaged to another girl already – but I couldn't let Paro down. Of course we couldn't work it out together, but one thing about Paro, life is never boring with her around – only a little too interesting, ha ha.'

My heart had curled up like a rosebud at the mention of B.R.'s name. I tried to hide my agitation from Suresh; we stopped for a paan and then dropped Bucky home. He was quite high and we waited while he fumbled long and unsurely with the doorbell, and a bleary servant opened the door.

We were silent all the way home, each lost in our private thoughts – I didn't even try to fathom what Suresh's were. The intimacy of our early married years, where we shared, if nothing else, the thrill of social battle, had quite disappeared. Then we had that brief interlude of happiness which was shattered by my abortion. Now we were two separate people; we knew each other's habits intimately; but losing the baby had left painful, indelible scars on both of us, and we shared only our silences.

Late that night, when I lay deep in dreamless slumber, Suresh rolled over and pulled me towards him. My favourite fantasy starring B.R. snapped into subliminal operation, and I partook of groggy but intense sexual pleasure. 'Bubu, darling,' I murmured, nibbling delicately at his ears. He stiffened for a moment, and I was instantly on the alert, and slobbered even more enthusiastically over him. Of course, only Paro called B.R. Bubu, but I don't think he made the connection. I don't know myself why her endearments rose unbidden to my lips.

Lenin's parents and family came to Delhi for the shopping and things like that. They were pondering where to have the wedding. Perhaps the Prime Minister could be persuaded to attend in Delhi, but then, Paro might not be persuaded not to. They were horrified to find Lenin still as enslaved by her as ever, and they decided to have the ceremonies in their home town.

Suresh was quite determined to go to Ramnagar, but then he got a very important and prestigious brief, which was likely to be heard the day of the wedding. Suresh was undecided, weighing the pros and cons – the contacts against the fees against the prestige; in the balance was also, I think, some genuine affection. All said and done, Lenin was one of the nicest people we had encountered over the years, a genuine friend, and, in spite of his often vitriolic outbursts, completely harmless.

Suresh was still wavering when Lenin's father asked if he could come over. I had never met him before. He was as unlike Lenin as anybody could possibly be; as fat as Lenin was thin, as crude as he was subtle, as pompous as he was casual. After all these years, his bucolic origins had not yet rubbed off – I suppose they were an essential prop in his political persona.

He was direct and to the point. 'That bloody beetch insists on coming for the wedding,' he said. 'If you attend, she will definitely come as well. Try to make sure she doesn't come, Suresh Babu.'

Suresh was looking worried. He couldn't very well say no, but I could see him pondering the difficulties of stopping Paro from doing anything she had set her mind upon. But I must admit that Suresh's style in dealing with an ex-minister who might conceivably become important again was a masterly exercise in condescending humility. It was an entirely non-verbal exposition, and yet contained within it a complicated social statement. It was indeed by his excessive politeness that he conveyed the concession he was making to past glory.

Lenin's sister from Jabalpur, who was in Delhi with her family, telephoned me. I invited her to a kitty party. She had lunch with me later, and told me in anxious detail about how worried her family was about Lenin's behaviour, what high hopes they had always nurtured for Lenin, how good and bright he had been as a child, and how very shocked and hurt her would-be bhabhi would be if she came to know of the extent of Lenin's involvement with Paro.

'I am sure she has done some tantric magic on him, otherwise why should my brother even look at that old hag?' she asked knowingly, nodding her head from side to side. I agreed heartily. She told me again about how rich the girl's family was, and about how she was sure everything would settle down after the wedding.

Suresh dealt with Paro simply, and in a straightforward manner. 'Look, Paro,' he said, 'they simply don't want you there. You can go and make a fool of yourself – or you can stay behind and prove you are not bothered.'

Paro looked around confusedly, evading direct eye contact. 'Lenin wants me to,' she said defiantly.

'Don't be silly, Paro,' Suresh said, exasperated. 'Or, if you want to be, do as you please.'

She seemed to be having an internal dialogue. She sat still and pensive for a while, looking very thin and resolute. Then suddenly she smiled. 'Don't be silly, yaar. The country hicks will stare at me like somebody from a zoo. Let Priya go and represent all of us,' she said flippantly.

So I was dispatched to Ramnagar, in the heart of eastern U.P., to represent them at the wedding. Lenin looked terribly lost in the midst of all that nuptial splendour. His family had persuaded him to shave off his beard, and he looked thinner than ever, and very incongruous in shiny gold and brocade. He kept fumbling awkwardly with his heavy gold mukut, which would constantly slip down his forehead. His wife was very beautiful. Fair, clean-looking, her hair reaching till her knees, shyly radiant in hymenal red, she looked every inch a bride. I remembered what a defiant, different sort of bride Paro had been, and felt old for the first time in my life.

Everyone was excessively nice to me. They even gave me an expensive silk sari, and all the respect and attention due to Lenin's Rakhi sister. I felt somehow very comfortable and at home amongst the crowded, happy guests and relatives. Some of the local women tried to question me about Paro and Lenin and Delhi. 'People there are very advanced,' they said wistfully, 'they don't believe in marriage sharriage or anything any more.'

Paro sent a telegram; but her ghost was nowhere present in the garish happiness around us. Laddoos were distributed to the whole town, and the day after the wedding there was a mujra for the bridal couple, organised by the bride's brother, who owned a sugar mill and a chain of cold storages. I got a lot of uncomplicated pleasure in dressing up in heavy wedding clothes, and flaunting all the jewellery I had accumulated over the years. Quite to my satisfaction, I had been assigned the role of the sophisticate from Delhi. In fact, some people even mistook me for Paro, and would point and stare at me and whisper speculatively to each other, probably about what strange and mysterious magic I could have exercised over Lenin.

The mujra was quite nice. There was a thin young girl, dressed somewhere between a sleazy cabaret artiste and Anarkali, who performed a provocative dance. Lenin and his wife were seated on a dais, on golden chairs with a peacock emblem. They were resplendent. Lenin looked like a young prince from a mythological film, and sat drumming some obscure tune with his thin fingers on the arm of the golden peacock chair, which had been specially brought from Calcutta. His wife, who sat beside him, was just a blur of gold, rubied diamonds and flowers. There was a great crowd of people all around, looking sweaty and excited in the harsh floodlights. Mosquitoes attended by the millions, but they seemed to bother nobody except me and Lenin, perhaps because of our fresh city blood. He kept scratching tormentedly during the ceremonies, and I too was in agony throughout, and the pale pink of my nails kept getting stained a deep vicious red from the blood of dead mosquitoes.

When I returned to Delhi after the wedding, covered with mosquito bites, life seemed dull and blank. Paro was again without a man in her life; there was a stillness, a lull, stagnation. Suresh was busier than ever before, and each day stretched cavernous and empty before me.

A friend of mine had a small bookshop in the Oberoi Hotel. She asked me if I wanted a part-time job, and I agreed eagerly. It was a quiet, peaceful place, and I would spend hours, curled up in a corner, leafing through books and magazines. Occasionally a customer would stroll in, and I would rise, show him around, and settle down to my private thoughts again.

I grew to love that little bookshop. I revelled in its beige-carpeted highbrow atmosphere, and in its absence of malice. Suresh was very upset at my taking up a job. 'Priya, think of my position in society. Why people will think – doesn't her husband earn enough for both of them for her to take such a job?'

But I was unmoved, for that job represented escape from my empty home. Of course, it wasn't my first job either, for I had put in three years of service with Sita Sewing Machines. It was pleasant to earn some money again, however little it might be. I worked from nine-thirty in the mornings, when Suresh left for court, until four in the afternoons, at which time he normally returned. I was paid a thousand rupees a month. I never spent any of the money on myself, since personal maintenance and so on I took to be my legal due from Suresh; instead it accumulated in my personal account, a little nest-egg of my own. I think I deserved it, even if I do say so myself, for I was very conscientious about the cash box, and even put an end to all the pilfering that had been rampant earlier.

I would sit perched on the precarious little chair behind the cigarette counter, and look enquiringly, even frostily, at the customers (mostly firangs) who came for the foreign editions of papers, or in search of touristy guide books, or to ask about the occasional fake antique or Tankha we would place in the shop window.

I had always loved books and started reading voraciously again. I began at one corner of the shop and carefully waded my way through a random and eclectic sea of information. I would start on Indian Art, and move to Indian Cookery, erotic prints from Japan, how Bonington scaled the Himalayas; even, when their time came, through almost the entire range of pornographic titles, which we kept discreetly hidden behind the first row of books. (These I always read enfolded within the pages of some respectable magazine.) Then I would move on to the Silhouette romances, or *A Shorter History of India*, and so on.

I always read the books very carefully, never opening them flat, and being otherwise very careful not to damage the spines. I would read only the first page of foreign newspapers so as not to disturb the folds, and consequently became very conversant with the major issues confronting the modern world, and a lot of socio-cultural details I had never been aware of. But I stopped at the front-page news. However tempting it might be to continue to page five, or seven, I would never do so for fear of spoiling the clear virgin folds.

One day I looked up from page one of the International Herald Tribune. It was, I still remember, full of lovely details about the Royal Wedding, and I was wondering whether to continue to page three or stick by my principles when suddenly a presence hovered before me. I knew in my deepest instincts who it was. Besides, the smell of the aftershave was heart-rendingly familiar. My eyes levelled to a paunchy midriff valiantly held back by a tight lizard-skin belt. A soft, hirsute stomach showed through the snapping buttons. Two buttonholes up, I met a salt and pepper chest, generously exposed, and with faint mammary projections.

I should not speak so irreverently of my beloved, for it was he, B.R., Managing Director of Sita Sewing Machines Ltd, The Associated Machinery Corporation Private Ltd, and now the Milan Mixi range of household goods. 'The Housewife's Friend' was how his advertising campaigns still read, for I encountered them, often enough, in the morning papers and the glossies, and it was indeed the Housewife's Friend who stood before me.

'Why, Priya, what a wonderful surprise!' he exclaimed in his immaculate Oxbeas accent, his face beaming with genuine pleasure at the sight of me.

'I can't leave the shop until four,' I stammered unasked, then blushed at my gaffe.

'Oh, marvellous,' he replied, 'I shall be in my room after that. I'm leaving by the evening flight. You must come up for some coffee.'

I was silent, speechless.

'You will, won't you, darling Priya,' he pleaded, and I could not but relent. He left after buying himself some papers, leaving me flustered and in a state of utter consternation. Although it weighed on my conscience, I bunked the shop and disappeared downstairs to the beauty parlour for a quick hairset; I was, if I say so myself, quite well preserved for my thirty-odd years. A quick dab of lipstick and blush on, and I was quite ready to take on the world.

I left the shop on the dot of four. B.R. was talking on the telephone when I entered.

'So, boss, how's the sex life?' I asked saucily, breezing into the room. Well, I intended it to sound pert, and funny; but as the words left my Kiss 'n' Tell lipsticked lips they sort of collapsed, and I ended up sounding sarcastic, defensive, even bitter. Perhaps I hadn't admitted to myself how much I missed him. And now here, in his enveloping presence, I felt so complete somehow, so safe, so cherished, so beloved.

B.R. had just returned from Europe. He was full of impressive statistics about export figures and quite poetic about the Eastern Bloc markets, and rupee trade, and other such conversation that made me feel truly a woman of the world. 'But these Delhi-wallahs,' he said, 'they want a finger in every pie. The trouble with India is that we are a nation of middlemen. Still, I always prefer to land in Delhi when I come in. When I land in Bombay the drive from the airport really hits me. It's a real culture shock! One always forgets the stink!

'And how's Paro?' he asked. 'I heard that Lenin character has run off and got married? So she's alone again, is she?' There was too much complacency and self-satisfaction in his voice for any spite to penetrate; but I felt it lurked beneath the surface, somewhere.

I don't know why I rose to her defence. 'Paro is a beautiful person, in her way,' I said, 'and if you had stayed married to her, and not womanised so much, both of you would have been happier people!'

He looked amused. 'Speaking for myself, I don't really seek or deserve more happiness than I have already got. As for womanising, I love women; I always have and I always will. But,' he continued, his voice assuming a certain self-righteous timbre, 'I've never paid for a woman in my life. I've never been to a whore or a prostitute! And I'm proud of it!'

'Do you love me, B.R.?' I asked timidly.

'Not only do I love you, but I also like you, my dear,' he said indulgently. 'You are real, you are honest, you are intelligent and undemanding.' He patted my hand fondly, and I blushed with pleasure.

I went to the bathroom to cover my embarrassment. I saw my face in the bathroom mirror; and I looked beautiful. I know I don't look like that every day. Perhaps it was love.

I was feeling so warm and flushed that I bent down to splash some cold water on to my face. As I was repairing my makeup, I noticed the dozens and dozens of bottles and tubes of creams and lotions and perfumes lined like toy soldiers around the sink. There was a silver hairbrush with greying hair entwined around it, and a grimy comb. I had never before realised the extent of his vanity.

We had some coffee after that, and pastries. And we talked; we discussed the weather, and Bubbles, and Hindi films, and things like that.

'And how is Suresh?' he asked. Perhaps he enquired only conversationally, but it was so rare for anyone to really talk to me that I burst out with a detailed critique of Suresh and our sterile, loveless life together. I was surprised by my own eloquence and clarity. It arose, I think, out of trust, for I even told him about the abortion.

B.R. listened to me patiently. He didn't mock, nor was he bored, he merely listened. Even before I was through with my long incoherent tirade, I knew that I had said nothing at all. Yet all my pent-up loneliness found relief, and gratitude and love jostled in my small heart. Afterwards, we had more coffee, and I had a pastry. I left at five thirty. We exchanged only a platonic peck upon parting, but my swooning lips carried the bristling impress of his fragrant cheeks for a long time.

When I reached home, Suresh glanced suspiciously at my flushed appearance, but refrained from any comment. Life went on. We hardly ever met Paro. In fact, we hardly ever met anyone, except on weekends, for Suresh had more work than he could cope with. He had several juniors working with him in his chambers now.

Lenin's wedding was, in many ways, a watershed in all our lives. The separate rhythms of all our lives no longer had any real meeting-ground. Suresh kept getting busier and busier. He was frequently out of town. I rarely accompanied him. I had certain shrewd suspicions about Uma, his sexy-looking junior, who accompanied him sometimes, ostensibly to help him with his briefs. But I knew Suresh too well to harbour any serious doubts, for he was basically a staid and dependable man. In a way, I was perhaps too enervated to even care, and so the green-eyed monster received very little sustenance, in spite of warning noises from several supposed friends and well-wishers.

Lenin's wedding, and the passage of years, was beginning to show upon Paro as well, and not only emotionally. A fretwork of fine lines framed the corners of her eyes and lips, and her skin had the slight tautness that heralds the advent of the middle years. Perhaps it was only a dry winter skin; but she looked so pale, so unlike herself, that I felt almost protective.

We met, of all places, at a vegetable shop in Defence colony. It was a Saturday, and I was buying some gladioli for a small dinner party we were having at home that evening. She was – unimaginable scenario – buying vegetables – onions, potatoes, tomatoes – feeling them for firmness, even checking the prices. She was dressed in a white khaddar kurta-pyjama. Her hair was oiled and tied into a loose plait, her face was devoid of make-up, and yet something in her made the shopkeeper bow and scrape and run devotedly to her bidding. I had stepped out of a chauffeured car; I was resplendent in a light floral chiffon; Y.S.L. goggles nestled on the bridge of my nose; I resented the attention she so effortlessly commanded.

She was unexpectedly friendly, and asked after Suresh, saying she wanted to consult him about some problems she was facing. Could she drop by the next morning to take his advice? Of course she must drop by, I replied effusively, and yes, of course I would tell Suresh to expect her.

She came bright and early the next morning, swaddled in a large pashmina shawl, her eyes outlined starkly with black eyeliner. Suresh had gone for a conference, and I told her he would be back soon.

'Will you have some coffee, Paro?' I asked.

'I want lemon tea,' she replied airily. 'I'm on a strict diet. I have to lose some of this flab around my hips, you know, for Clytemnestra.'

I looked blank.

'Aeschylus,' she elucidated. 'The trilogy. It's in translation, for the Hindustani theatre festival. I play Clytemnestra. The heroine,' she added unnecessarily.

Abruptly, she changed the subject. 'You're looking, sort of younger, more alive, Priya,' she said beguilingly. 'It must be your lovely job, all those books. Oh, it's really essential to have something to pour one's energies into.'

I looked suspiciously for the inevitable quid pro quo, for I did not flatter myself that Paro would waste time being nice to me without some more insidious motivation.

All she wanted was to pump me about the wedding. 'You poor child, Lenin's wedding must have been such a bore,' she began disarmingly.

I did not take the cue, and told her in excruciating detail about how beautiful Lenin's wife was, and how he had taken to matrimony like a duck to water. I went into rhapsodies over what was a slightly exaggerated account of the magnificence of the wedding.

'But of course he married her for her dowry,' she murmured, 'the dear bourgeois boy! You poor darling, all these mosquito bites! I'm so glad I didn't go.'

'They've healed now,' I said defensively.

'Lenin told me,' she continued, 'that he'd be back the day I so much as snap my fingers for him. These small-town girls are so boring, after a while. He did it on the rebound, of course.'

I thought of the firm set of his wife's chin, and of her father, and her large, determined family, but I did not voice my thoughts, for I could see that it was important to Paro to interpret her position thus.

She was all this while fingering a huge, ruby-studded pendant, set in gold, and shaped like a bird in flight, which straddled her long shapely neck. She fumbled with the clasp, and gave it to me to admire. The craftsmanship was really exquisite. It was beautiful, but a little bizarre, and I knew nobody who could have carried it off except Paro.

'Open it, yaar, it's a pendant,' she said impatiently. I did as commanded, and found something engraved in minute italicised letters across the wingspan. I squinted closer. It read: 'It is certain that fine women eat a crazy salad with their meat.' I pondered what exactly it meant.

'A wedding present,' she said smugly, 'from Lenin.'

'Tell me about the play,' I said, cursing Paro for never allowing me the privilege of pity.

'Oh, I'm doing it in an attempt to, you know, find myself. I mean, I've spent the last umpteen years fucking the men in my life, and getting fucked myself in the process.'

I wondered if she meant it literally or figuratively.

'And so, one day, after Lenin had left, and I was all alone in the flat, I looked at myself in the mirror. "Who are you, Paro?" I asked myself. And I knew I didn't know. So I started looking for myself again, deciding to follow wherever my search took me.'

She made it sound like a treasure-hunt.

'And so I joined this way-out encounter group. It was full of, you know, these fat-cat businessmen and some arty types. All prima donnas with problems, who could afford to bleed at the pocket for this chic psychiatrist. So I went there, and let my hair down, and screamed it all out about my traumas and things. But I found that most of these types were just sitting tight and watching.

They didn't let go at all. All they wanted to do was make out with me. Seems their primal problem was that they needed a good fuck. Every night, somebody would be asking me out for dinner, or propositioning me without even the preliminaries. Even the bloody psychiatrist. And if there's one thing I'm certainly not on to these days,' she shuddered theatrically, 'it's men. That's one scene I don't need, thank you very much.'

'You were telling me about the play,' I said patiently.

'Aah, that. There's this guy – he's a queer, don't worry, a brilliant young director called Krishen Narain Singh. I bet even you've heard of him.'

I confessed that I had.

'Well, he met me around, and started raving about what a beautiful speaking voice I had, and how there was theatre in my every movement. At first I thought he was trying to lay me, but he does that only to the male leads. He's very moody with women. He finds it difficult to really emote with them, and he was desperate for the right Clytemnestra. So I went for a few auditions, and I found that I really identified, like, with this woman. I sort of empathise, you know, all the contradictions in my own life. This Clytemnestra is a passionate and strong woman, with this creepy husband. So she kills him. So her son kills her. Krishen explained it to me, it's all these male types, it's because of the social framework. You know, all the fucking freedom of men, and none for women; so she has no other outlet for her frustrated intelligence. She's a very enigmatic character,' she concluded complacently, 'just like me.

'You must come and see me, both of you. You'll love it. It's in Hindi, Hindusthani really, more colloquial, you know, there's no real audience for the English stuff,' she continued knowledgeably. Then she started off militantly about men again, and what shits they were. 'The trouble with this goddamn country is that all the men want only one thing,' she sighed.

Just then Suresh returned. Success had made his portly figure, earlier the butt for so many jokes, look almost acceptable. 'Just a few minutes, Priya, and then we'll be with you,' he said, like a dentist to a patient, and whisked Paro away to his chamber. They came down more than an hour later, and the three of us had a quiet lunch together. Paro even complimented me upon my cooking.

Suresh was extremely impressed with the idea of our Paro acting in a play.

'She really is a very talented girl,' he kept repeating. He would constantly punctuate his pompous and repetitive store of jokes and anecdotes with wondering, besotted references to Paro. 'She really is a very talented girl,' he would sigh, 'she just needs expression for her talent.'

I even saw him leafing through a library copy of the play; but it seemed to bore him and he soon gave up. I read through it, though, in a copy I found at the bookshop.

Paro was coming over regularly again. Yet another problem had surfaced in her teeming life – a distant one, but all the more alluring for its lack of immediate impact upon her personally. Her Keralite ayah, Maryamma, who had brought Junior up, adored her uncompromisingly. In fact, Maryamma refused to leave Paro even after her arranged marriage to a prosperous chauffeur in Dubai. Every now and then he would return to India to herd a few more relatives back with him; but there was a tacit understanding that Maryamma could never abandon her mistress for him. Raju would inundate her with saris, watches, tape recorders and an endless flow of passionate letters full of romantic allusions to popular Hindi film songs. Maryamma, lonely amidst all the electronic largesse, would read these letters out to Paro, who derived an immense deal of malicious glee at Raju's articulation of his ardour.

Raju didn't write for a long time, and Maryamma was anxious and worried. Then one of her brothers came to see her. Paro returned home one afternoon to find Maryamma in hysterics.

'All finished, Madame, all finished,' she cried. But the brother had disappeared and Paro could extract nothing further from Maryamma, who couldn't stop her tears and kept repeating, 'All finished Madame, all finished.'

What we could piece together, finally, was that Raju had been involved in some kind of lafda with his mistress.

'Very bad, these Arab ladies very bad, Madame,' Maryamma would repeat piteously. 'The Master,' on uncovering the lafda, confiscated the year's salary he always kept in reserve, gave Raju back his passport and return fare to India. This was more than two months ago, and no one had heard of him since, on either end.

Paro energetically if somewhat haphazardly undertook to trace the missing Raju. She accosted Suresh and demanded he file a case.

'On what grounds?' he asked.

'Habeas Corpus,' she replied importantly, and he could not, I think, properly convey to her his inability to take any legal action for, besotted as he was, any threadbare excuse to meet Paro was better than life without her.

She even telephoned the Foreign Secretary, and when he pleaded his inability to 'do anything concrete' she went to meet the Pakistani ambassador, who was her 'yaar'.

But Raju could not be traced, and Maryamma wouldn't eat anything and took to just sitting around, staring at the walls. For a few days Paro tended Maryamma devotedly but then got tired of declaiming and posturing as Clytemnestra over a sinkful of dirty dishes; household work irked her. She would drop by for lunch and dinner whenever she wasn't going out, which was often, as she wasn't feeling social.

So I got to hear a lot of transliterated Aeschylus, in a shrill convent Hindi, and a daily bulletin on Raju's continued and mysterious disappearance and Maryamma's emotional state.

She presented us with four front-row passes for the opening performance of the play. We went with the Johoreys, who were a very cultivated and cultured couple, and as such likely to appreciate the play. It was a beautiful evening, and the hall was packed with beautiful and elegant people, and I felt beautiful to be part of such a beautiful world. On stage, the lighting was harsh and frontal, and everything stood out almost in relief.

Everybody in the play was dressed in flowing black, and the sets too consisted of what appeared to be large black packing cases, which cunningly became now the throne, now a silver bathtub or a ship of war. I discovered to my surprise that Clytemnestra was not by any account the heroine of the play; in spite of all her clear scornful looks and proud demeanour, I felt Paro certainly couldn't call herself the heroine. And she certainly wasn't right in carrying on with another man and killing her husband, and I thought her son was quite justified in getting provoked enough to kill her.

Paro was a surprisingly good actress. She had power and presence, and the only fault, to my middle-class Vividh-Bharati ears, lay perhaps in her imperceptibly anglicised enunciation, of what she so emphatically deemed 'Hindustani'.

During the interval, Suresh insisted that he wanted some coffee and popcorn. In the crowded marble lobby we met Bucky Bhandpur, with Junior, who was down from Doon for his vacations. He was as thin as ever, and he had grown even taller. Except for the shining metal braces on his teeth (which protruded like Bucky's) he had grown into a startlingly handsome young man. Affection welled unbidden in my heart, for his dazzling youthful vulnerability. Clumsily and uncharacteristically, I reached out to stroke his long thick unkempt hair, and he recoiled shyly. Bucky seemed very fond of him, and was quite transformed by his new-found paternal role.

They too were in the front row, but at the other end. I was curious about how Junior (for that was how I still thought of him) would respond to the complex and slightly ambiguous theme, and I searched through the crowd of faces, craning my neck to do so, till my gaze settled on his young rapt face as he watched his mother. Such unquestioning adoration, such love and joy, seeped through his countenance that I was enchanted, and spent the rest of the evening watching not the play but him.

We went backstage after the play was over. Paro was breathing heavily, and perspiration beaded her brows. She was radiant from her success and continued offstage to emanate the sense of power and presence she had conveyed in her interpretation of the role. It was a sort of hangover – the mannerisms, movements, and some intrinsic self-image clung on like a strong perfume, and were to stay, in fact, for years, till the bitter end. Suresh had sent a basket of yellow roses ahead, and she gave him a grave kiss on his cheek to thank him. Bhandpur and Junior hovered around the crowded dressing-room. They were all going out for dinner together, and although Bucky asked us to join them, they looked so much the happy nuclear family that we had not the heart to intrude.

Suresh was progressing steadily at his legal career. He did better and better everyday; all the years of assiduous cultivation, of contacts, of reading endless briefs, seemed finally to be paying off. We saw less and less of each other, and met at weekend dinner parties, or across the silent dining table, at breakfast and dinnertime at home. I couldn't sleep well, somehow, and whenever I awoke at night, to drink water or go to the bathroom, the rhythmic complacent music of his snores would awaken in me an almost murderous irritation.

The bookshop and the job didn't seem so exciting any more. At home, I was caught up in the unending trivia of housekeeping. Whenever we went out, the ladies and gents seemed inevitably to be seated at polar ends of the room, to meet only at the dinner table, or if we were at a restaurant, at the dance floor where the bravest among us would go to shake a leg. I loved to waltz, but was quite hopeless at modern dancing. It was Suresh who had, to my surprise, blossomed into the dancer of the family. His self-confidence had increased beyond all recognition, and he would inevitably lumber over to the youngest and prettiest member of the group and formally request a dance. The sight of his lugubrious frame swaying in slightly unsynchronised rhythm to the already discordant music provoked a great deal of good-natured laughter. In our group, Suresh's dancing was always a ready cue for a giggle – a tension breaker, a ready change of subject when conversations veered towards rocky ground.

Suresh had been announcing his intentions of taking off to Bangkok for a relaxed weekend for a long time now. He kept cracking stupid jokes about friends: 'Jinhone Thailand mein ladki to Pattaya.' I wanted to go too, but he giggled and told me that going to Bangkok with a wife was like taking sandwiches to a restaurant.

But his programme kept getting delayed or postponed due to various reasons, until, one week, when there were a lot of court holidays, he did finally manage to make a getaway. I sat alone at home; it was a Sunday morning. I realised suddenly that I was quite alone in the world. I had nobody, but nobody, who loved me, liked me, or even cared for me. I had a host of acquaintances – my kittyparty friends, all of whom despised me with the same intensity with which they disliked each other; Atul Bhaiya, whose wife didn't like me in the least, and who wrote me a token cheque every Rakshabandhan; Lenin, who had sent me a postcard once from Paris; and B.R., who, paired with Paro, still figured as one of the twin divinities in my private mythology. And, of course, Paro herself, friendly, deceptively normal, enacting scenes from a cosy family life with Bucky – Paro, whose very existence made mine seem duller.

Even in the bookshop, the smell of new paper and all those clean glossy covers couldn't cheer me any more. I was tired, and bored, and exhausted with the effort of mindless survival. Reading had been a tortuous new experience, a sort of vision of unconfronted worlds. But my concentration was fragile, and I did not really have the courage to confront those battalions of words, and so I abandoned the habit of reading and the escape routes thereof. Immediately on returning from the shop I would fall into a heavy, drugged sleep, only to awake even more tired than ever. I felt constantly ill, and even found a doctor who pandered outrageously to my hypochondria, so that I was constantly benumbed by the consumption of millions of tablets and pills. My mental and physical states would co-relate to the degree of absorption of the various chemicals in my bloodstream, so that I was to all practical effect an absolute zombie.

One day I received a letter from the past; Mary wrote to me saying that her youngest brother had become a lawyer and was thinking of practising in Delhi. He wanted some introductions into the right legal circles, and, for old time's sake, would Suresh take him under his wing, or even, perhaps – the letter hinted – a junior, or perhaps a partner. It was a long and sentimental letter; Mary was now happily married and had four children. 'And how is our mad ex-bossreine?' it continued smugly. 'I heard that you are in touch with her. The big boss is still sighted around Bombay sometimes, hunting for all kinds of goodies to eat... but wifey number two is no longer in the kitchen, not that she ever was, ha ha! He is as gallant and dashing as ever – I know you had a soft spot for him in your sweet chocolate heart... does Suresh ever feel jealous, I wonder? [She had never met Suresh] You were always the brightest of all of us, we were all sure you would go really far in life; and indeed you have, with a lawyer husband in Delhi and all. You must look me up in Bombay, we'll have real fun and some good home-made food. I will give you genuine Goanese fare – my figure has become like Tun Tun with my own cooking, and as Robert is still as trim as ever, I have to be very careful to make sure that the way to his heart remains through his stomach.'

The constant references to digestive metaphors were really startling. It was, I was sure, more deep-rooted than just a quaint idiosyncrasy of style. All kinds of dreadful anal images crowded into my mind; I wondered about the routes to Suresh's heart, and mentally checklisted all his various orifices – his indifferent ears (he never listened to anything I ever said), his mouth, his stinking yellow teeth, his red cavernous tongue (I didn't ever want to kiss it), his hairy nostrils, his constricted constipated sphincter – and realised afresh how much I hated him. Mary's gregarious letter was like a vision, a reminder that in some distant world people were normal, friendly, relaxed, happy, cheerful – or so it seemed from this long chatty intimate letter. I wondered what kind of missive I could send in response, for she hadn't met me in years. I could construct any façade, conjure any reality, for her, and it would have a validity at least in the writing.

I sat and composed letters by the score. 'Dear Mary, I was pleasantly surprised to get your letter… you know what a busy schedule I keep' … 'Dear Mary, I'm sorry I don't really remember your name or face from my office days, it was all so very long ago' … 'Dear Mary, who exactly did you see B.R. with?' … 'Dear Mary, how do you have the energy and assurance to write such a letter to a total stranger?' … 'Dear Mary, I saw Paro yesterday and I am as much in love with her as ever' … 'Dear Mary, Robert sounds a real shit and Suresh is trying very hard to get it up in Bangkok.'

That letter probably saved me from a nervous breakdown. I wrote and rewrote torrents of letters, and, predictably, posted none. But I started a sort of confessional, a diary, which eventually became this thing, this novel.

I would write everywhere, in my sleep, over my morning tea, hunched over the commode, in the shop, in the crevices of my mind under Suresh's incurious, unseeing stare. I covered sheet after sheet with my neat spiky handwriting and watched astounded as it emerged in bursts and dribbles. Sometimes it dried up altogether, only to secrete in some corner of my subconscious, and pour out again in random recognitions of my, and her, life.

I had always considered myself a person of little consequence, and less talent. I discovered, however, that I had an instinct, a faculty, for truth. I saw things as they were, not as they should have been or people tried to pretend they were. It was this faculty for truth that had haunted me for years, distorting the happiest moments of my life, mocking love, happiness, security. Even amidst the deepest possible flow of emotions I could never abandon the unmoved voyeur within me, the wary spectator in the crowd, never participating, only watching.

I scribbled on the backs of envelopes, on notepads, with my eyebrow pencil on the back of a letter; anything to contain the flood of memories when the dam broke. Sometimes I would wake up in the far reaches of the night and gently dislodge myself from bed so as not to disturb snoring Suresh. I would stumble in the dark towards his office chamber and extort each painful truth with practised secretarial fingers on his heavy grumbling typewriter.

Obviously all this feverish activity could not be kept

secret for long. I will not flatter myself and think that Suresh sensed any of my inner turmoil, but he did sense my increasing inattentiveness, and the clatter of the typewriter, the scattered pages, did arouse his suspicions. 'What are you up to, little woman?' he enquired bluffly. 'Oh, just some old cookery recipes,' I parried. I could well foresee, and certainly did not want to face, the ridicule were my secret ever to out.

But out it did. Inevitably it was my nemesis Paro who came prying into my bedroom one day. She had come to consult with Suresh about one or other of her cases. She suddenly 'got her chums', as she inelegantly explained later. So she went looking for some sanitary towels in my cupboard drawer, where she 'just happened' to chance upon a sheaf of papers, and again 'just chanced' to look through them. At first she couldn't quite catch the trend of it, but it obviously held her attention, for it was only after a good half-hour's read that she found herself possessed by a towering quivering all-consuming rage and stalked out to confront me.

'You leech,' she screamed, 'you neuter, your lifeless zombie, you peeping pisspot, why don't you shed your own blood for a change!' Suresh appeared, alarmed by all the shouting, and posted himself uncertainly at the door. 'Read this,' she said, hammering at his chest, 'the stupid bitch is trying to write about me!' So Suresh settled himself on the sofa and began reading. Paro poured herself a stiff whisky soda and settled down next to Suresh, reading his face and graphing his expressions as he leafed through the pages.

Suresh read for a very long time, during which Paro alternated between mockery and anger. 'You sneak,' she would hiss, 'you little spy, you bloody lesbo, you don't even have the guts to live your own bloody life, always creeping about me and Bubu… tell me, who turns you on more, me or your darling B.R.? Hah, B.R., that miserable prick, hah!'

Suresh looked sterner and sterner. I felt hysterical with anger and relief – anger that they were mocking my book; relief that they were reading it.

I was very nervous, with a sort of stagefright, the apprehension, perhaps, of some drama in my own life. Finally Suresh got up, very quietly, and took off his reading glasses, gently stroking the bridge of his nose with his podgy index finger. Even the rocking chair halted to attention.

'My dear Priya, this is a very serious matter,' he said, in his deliberate lawyer's voice. The lurking hysteria finally overpowered me. I noticed that I was giggling nervously. That seemed to unsettle him, but it provoked Paro even more. She came over to the velvet upholstered pouffe where I was sitting, doubled over with suppressed laughter. Suddenly, her soft, perfumed hands were buffeting me right and left, and I was enveloped by darkness, before the stars began shining. Suresh's chair began rocking with some weird momentum of its own as my pouffe collided with it, skeetering off towards the door.

But a livid Paro held me back, spitting surrogate viscous tears down my cheeks, pulling at my hair like an avenging fury. Clumps and locks of hair lay strewn about me as though in some strange autumnal rite. There were five burning red welts on my cheek, where she had lashed at me with those soft perfumed fingers. 'You voyeur… you… you vicarious bitch,' she whispered into my smarting ears, and spat venomously at the hair that still lay limply in her hands.

Suresh watched, a little astonished, while I screamed with pain and humiliation. But he did nothing to interfere; in fact, he seemed rather to be enjoying it.

'My dear Priya,' he began again, clearing his throat importantly, 'this seems a rather… serious matter.'

Although I was still wincing with pain, I composed myself in a posture of mock-serious attention.

'Writing about us like this is something, which, to my mind, no Hindu housewife would ever do. And I must say, you don't seem to like us overmuch. In fact you have made fun of me. And as for your relationship with B.R.' – he coughed embarrassedly – 'is it… uh' – he looked to Paro for support – 'is it, fictional or, uh, factual?'

'Oh, she's been fucking him in her fantasies ever since I've known her,' Paro said spitefully, 'but I know she's not his type – he goes for, you know, more classy women; after all, he was my husband!'

That settled it. 'You stupid woman,' I said clearly, 'every word that I have written about you is the truth, the whole truth, and nothing but the truth. B.R. loves me and he's loved me for years, much before he even knew you, in fact.

'And if you think,' I said, turning my attention to Suresh, 'if you think I ever had, or could have had, any sentiment except... no, not hatred, you're not even worthy of that... if you think I could have had any sentiment for you except ridicule – then you are just an egotistical fool; I've lived with you like a whore, because you paid for it.'

Immediately, I felt sorry for my outburst. Suresh's face fell; he seemed genuinely hurt and shocked. 'But, Priya, you were my wife,' he said abjectly, 'I always thought we were happy together.'

Paro looked gleeful and triumphant, and suddenly I realised that we had, indeed, been happy together, in our way. I wanted to kiss him, or hold him, or somehow reassure him of my faith and trust, but Paro came between us.

'You really can't continue to be married to this first-class bitch, Suresh,' she said agitatedly, beginning to work herself into a rage again. 'How dare she sleep with my husband, how dare she how dare she how dare she!' And then, another transformation overtook her; she sort of arched herself seductively, and draped herself around a confused Suresh. 'Dearest, darling Suresh,' she cooed, looking deep into his eyes, 'you've always loved me, haven't you? All these years that you've kept silent...' She settled a long passionate kiss upon him; he was passive, transfixed. Then she undid her hair, and settled her cheek next to his. Her pallav fell off her shoulders, and her breasts were bared almost to the nipples. Amidst all the strange things that were happening, the sexual atmosphere in the room became suddenly almost palpable. Both Suresh and I could feel the vibrations, the tremors of guilty excitement. Her passion was very literal, that way, almost pornographic. She always used it as an instrument of warfare, to further her ends.

I felt tired, and nauseated, and disgusted, and defeated. 'I'm leaving,' I said, and carefully gathered the scattered sheets of my diary and put them into a plastic shopping bag. Then I walked out, closing the door gently behind me.

I walked out of my home all right, but I didn't know anywhere I could go to. I hadn't met B.R. for ages; my mother was dead; my brother's wife didn't like me; I didn't have any other friends, relatives or lovers. I walked around the park outside our house for a while, then sat down on a bench there. My book lay, dissembling, like a bag of knitting, at my feet. The full round moon shone behind the trees; the park looked beautiful, enchanting, magical. A cricket sang insistently in the hedges, and I felt strong, and whole, and not at all upset.

In a while I discovered I needed to go to the toilet. After a little hesitation I decided to go home. After all, I couldn't do it out there in the open. A drunk had teetered into the park and lain himself down on the damp grass at the other end. Soft snatches of not untuneful song wafted across the magical night.

I went back home and rang the doorbell. Nobody answered. I wondered where Ratan Singh was and walked in, for the door was not locked, and peeped in cautiously through the lobby door. They sat huddled together, in the dark dim drawing-room. A soft light was glowing from the lamp on the corner table; there was the soft clink of whisky glasses. Paro sat gently stroking Suresh's hair. They looked very complete.

Just then, Ratan Singh entered through the dining-room door. Instinctively, with a snooper's reflexes, I stiffened. Paro continued stroking Suresh's hair. She seemed not at all embarrassed. Neither, for that matter, did Ratan Singh. He enquired whether Sahib was ready for dinner. 'After a while,' Suresh replied, 'and I want parathas. Memsahib won't be back for dinner. Paro Madame khayengi.'

I should never have returned. But I barged into the room. 'Memsahib khayengi,' I said significantly. Suresh sat up embarrassedly. Paro was unperturbed. She continued to stroke his hair. I could feel Suresh turning red. After a while she withdrew her fingers, or rather her talons. Her eyes were narrowed in a familiar mocking way. All of us were silent. I went to the bathroom, returned, and poured myself a drink. Suresh walked over to the bar. 'Get me a drink as well, Suresh,' Paro cooed. Further silence. After a while I just left the room. I locked myself into our bedroom and shut the lights. Suresh did not knock all night; I was lonely without him.

Next morning I found him snoring gently on the drawing-room sofa. He looked clumsy and vulnerable, and a strange affection overcame me. He was a bumbling bully, but he was my husband. He awoke and gazed at me blearily, and didn't recall for some time that there was anything amiss. 'Tea, Priya,' he grunted, and turned over. Tenderly, I brought in the tea tray. Ratan Singh looked knowing.

After he had gulped down his tea, and his faculties had been somewhat restored, he stiffened and lapsed into his lawyer's voice again. 'I want a long discussion with you, Priya,' he said sternly.

I misgauged the moment. 'Of course!' I said gaily. 'No holds barred.'

'Have you really had a liaison with B.R.?' he asked.

'No, of course not,' I shuffled.

'Do you have any intention of trying to get that thing published?' he asked next.

That caught me unawares. I had not even considered the possibility. The idea floated like a magical bubble before me, enticing me with visions of glory, fame, even immortality. 'Yes,' I said, lost in my own dream world.

'And do you love B.R.?' he hammered unremittingly.

'Yes, yes,' I continued, still lost in my private rhapsody.

'In that case I think we would be best advised to live apart, at least for a while,' he said, and his voice had the ring of finality.

I realised I had been entrapped by cross-examining double-talk.

Before I could regain any lost ground, he was safe in the bathroom, and emerged fresh and squeaky clean in collar and coat, all ready for court. He worked his way carefully through a substantial breakfast before he left. I took a holiday from the shop, and dawdled about the empty house all day.

When he returned in the afternoon, his resolve had not faltered. 'I think it would be best for us to live apart for a while, Priya,' he said, quite gently.

I looked around; at my neat drawing-room, at the harmonious colours, the formal lines, the well tended potted plants. I was not going to forsake this haven. 'It is the only home I know,' I said stubbornly.

'But a separation cannot do us any harm,' he said, 'just to think matters over.'

'But where can I live? Even my mother's dead,' I said in desperation.

'There is always your brother's house,' he said. 'Or you can continue to live here, but then I shall have to shift out. And I do, after all, have to continue to live in Delhi to earn a living. My chambers and library are here. I have commitments to my clients.'

My tactless tongue flew loose again. 'What about maintenance, alimony?' I asked. The question of money was, after all, pressing and all-prevailing. Panic flew in waves around my head at the prospect of becoming Dolly's drudge, the object of pity, a poor relative.

My last question, about alimony, really got his goat. 'My dear Mrs Priya Kaushal,' he said grandiloquently, 'one thing you cannot, I repeat, cannot, accuse me of is ever even attempting, I repeat, even attempting, is to shirk or evade my responsibilities. I may be fat, I may even – in your eyes – be a buffoon, my love-making may leave you cold, but I do certainly abide by my duties. Even the fevered phantoms of your imagination cannot distort that irrefutable fact.' All this in his lawyer's voice. I could almost hear the choked 'M' Lord' at the edge of every plea. Perhaps beneath that lawyer's face he was, indeed, hurt. Perhaps in his way he did love me.

'I will arrange for your train booking for tomorrow,' he said, 'and inform your brother of your impending arrival.'

That did it. Even in this moment of passion he could not abandon his parsimony. 'I'll manage,' I said. 'I'll take a plane. I'll fly, and I'll buy the ticket myself.'

The next morning I telephoned Mrs Maira, who owned the bookshop, and was my proprietress, so to speak, and told her I was going on a few months' leave for pressing personal reasons. I then proceeded to my bank in a taxi and withdrew all my modest savings, leaving a balance of a few hundred rupees. I then went in the same grumbling taxi to the airlines office and bought myself a one-way ticket to Bombay. That left me with a little over twenty thousand in my purse. I felt secure, and even a little reckless. Upon reaching home, I packed all my best clothes very carefully into the blue Samsonite suitcase which Suresh had brought back from Bangkok. I checked Ratan Singh's accounts and told him I would be back in a month. 'Look after Sahib properly,' I said tonelessly, 'see that he eats properly.' This last admonition was actually a bit redundant, for Suresh's appetite seemed, if anything, only to have been whetted by a little domestic upheaval. Suresh telephoned Bhaiyya to inform him of my arrival, and drove me to the airport, and checked me in as well. He planted a formal peck on my cheek as I went into the security check, and then walked away, out of the airport. I felt alone, and not at all confident. Actually, I felt nothing, only numbed, and trusting only to memories of instincts and responses to get me through.

On the plane, the air-hostess gave me a kind smile and a sweet. I envied her self-possession and fumbled with my seat belt. The man sitting next to me courteously came to my aid. His hand brushed accidentally against my midriff and I felt a quiver of excitement, even arousal. I turned to thank him, effusively. His face was impassive and he seemed quite preoccupied, and he did not talk to me at all for the remainder of the flight.

As I walked towards the lavatory, I found a familiar figure seated in the front row. It was Shambhu Nath Mishra, in full ministerial regalia, with assistants and secretaries scattered all about him. He was dressed in his usual starched white dhoti and kurta, with an immaculate Gandhi topi perched atop his head – his spindly legs and fat torso, his whole presence, in spite of its innate comicality, still spelling power. I did an obsequious namaste.

'Aah… Priyaji,' he said, after a fraction's hesitation. 'How are you? Kyon, going to Bombay, kya?' I nodded. 'How is our Suresh? And your friend – or should I say our friend – Paro?' He smirked meaningfully. 'Please convey my regards to her,' he said, smirking again.

'Yes, yes, they are all fine,' I replied in a shrill foolish voice, and stumbled back to my seat in confusion. I got up again to go to the rear toilet, and my neighbour eyed me in mild surprise.

★

My sister-in-law, Dolly, was at the airport in Bombay to receive me. She was flanked by three children and a chauffeur. The chauffeur got my luggage out. I was glad it was a good-looking new suitcase. The children darted about me excitedly, and then the youngest, the boy, Prem, started crying. I tried unsuccessfully to hush him with a sweet. Dolly took no notice and marched us all into the car. Bhaiyya was not at home when we arrived; he was out of town and returning only the next day. In the evening, the children changed into pretty nighties and nightsuits and went into their ayah's arms. When they were asleep, the same ayah served us our dinner. I could not help but notice that her fingernails were filthy. The food, too, was heavy, pretentious and overcooked. Everything in the house was a strange mixture of tackiness and wealth. Dolly's hair was immaculately set in old-fashioned bangs that fell like perfectly geometrical musical notes about her face; she looked as though well-tended by the local beautician or health club; and yet the lacy strap of her bra, which kept escaping her blouse, was grimy and unwashed. Her neck was edged by the tidal marks of unwashed makeup, and my fastidiousness was utterly revolted.

A monsoon miasma of moisture and glistening wetness hung over everything. The pretty guestroom was musty and screamed for fresh air. The bedsheets stank of damp and disuse. I lay a sari over the bedsheet and slept through tired, troubled dreams.

By the next morning Bhaiyya was back. He was very affectionate, his personality had improved, and I was surprised to find that he was not quite the imbecilic twit that I remembered. There was, I imagine, some real affection exchanged between us, or perhaps it was just the commodity I was then hungriest for. He looked very smart and debonair and well-dressed. I had not seen him for almost five years now, and he had developed a startling resemblance to the old framed photograph of my father that my mother used to keep by her bedside. But he looked quite handsome, nevertheless.

'Daddy talks a lot about you,' Prem lisped, 'he says you were always very clever.' Dolly sniffed. 'After all, blood is deeper than water,' she said in somewhat shaky English. I realised suddenly that Bhaiyya alone, in all the world, was of my blood and flesh, and I felt a rush of love for him, and for my nephews and nieces seated around me. I wondered what it must be like to have children. Perhaps my marriage might even have been saved if I had children. I longed to hug Prem's angular limbs, to reassure his limpid eyes with my undying spinster-aunt love. I decided to endear myself to Dolly by taking charge of the children, and found to my surprise that they responded to my efforts.

Perhaps they were as starved for love as everyone else in our family. I took them to movies, and to ice cream parlours, and helped them with their homework. Dolly watched silently but said nothing. She would sniff at me suspiciously at mealtimes. She looked so like a well-fed cat, felinely licking at the chicken bones on her plate, that my composure would often desert me, and I would find myself breaking into light-headed giggles.

'What's so funny, Priya?' Bhaiyya would ask reprimandingly before reverting to his favourite subject of conversation, which was Dolly's father. He was obsessed by the man. Atul had given up on the medical profession in the process of marrying Dolly; and now managed her father's pharmaceutical business. Everything was 'Pappaji this', 'Pappaji that'. Dolly too referred every dispute or controversy to the arbitration of her absent 'Pappaji'. I was very eager and curious to meet him, and a little apprehensive about how he would grade me. He was however out on a world tour.

'I've asked Pappaji to get us some underwear and all from London – you know, Atul likes only flowered underwear from there,' she said confidingly. She pronounced it 'under-weeear', and followed it with a rhyming 'theeear'. My lips twitched. She sensed my passing attempt at social superiority, and grew suspicious again. The moment of womanly confidence had passed, and silence fell again.

Why didn't Dolly like me? For like me she didn't. Atul hinted as much, and tried to keep the peace, for theirs was, on the whole, a peaceable household. She was watchful and hostile, and unburdened her anger in private to Atul. 'Dolly thinks you're spoiling the children,' he said hesitantly one day. 'And then, Pappaji will be returning as well – I've been thinking, perhaps you'd like to live on your own in the Andheri flat.'

I was surprised, for I thought the Andheri flat had been disposed of on Mother's death. But Atul had apparently retained it as an investment and for unforeseen situations (amongst which he evidently classed me).

I did not relish being an inconvenience and so I shifted out the very next day.

I felt terrible at leaving the children, for I had grown fond of them, and needed the warmth of my nephew's trusting body to get me through the lonely nights. They were at school when I left; and I am sure that they missed me for a while.

The flat was just as I remembered, a journey inwards as well as into the past. I got down briskly to the immediate tasks of cleaning and dusting, for I did not have the strength nor the stomach for introspection; and soon it was inhabited by present as well as past ghosts. It was surprisingly comfortable and well maintained, and soon I felt as secure and habituated as if I had never moved out at all. I survived on black coffee and occasional meals, and spent most of my time reading. I even joined the local lending library, for I had to conserve funds until the situation clarified. Suresh had sent me a cheque for a reasonable amount, but he had not communicated with me in any other way. It was a strangely suspended sort of existence.

I discovered a cache of old books in a glass bookcase. There was my mother's collection of popular Hindi fiction, and carefully preserved copies of *Reader's Digest* lay in neat stacks beside a tattered copy of *Chiero's Palmistry*, which had belonged to my father. There was a yellowed copy of *Jane Eyre* from my schooldays. And then there was that beloved novel of my youth, *Rebecca*, with my maiden name inscribed in bright blue on the flyleaf.

Once again I abandoned myself to the fantasies of my youth. Only, rereading it now, I felt betrayed, utterly betrayed. Rebecca had, after all, done nothing wrong; the dazzlers in the new pulp paperbacks committed adultery almost as a rite of passage. Rebecca's only fault was that she was strong, stronger than Max! Not very profound observations, I am sure, but for me they held the blinding flash of revelation. My entire system of values was suddenly upturned. I felt a spiteful anger for that lying dog-eared novel, and wanted above all to tear it to smithereens and consign it to the dark monsoon sea.

Out of curiosity, and partly as a reaction, I started reading my mother's still intact library of Hindi Romance. Her taste had never been of the highest, and the paperbacks, stiff with age, were practically falling apart in my hands. It took some time for my eyes to readjust to the devnagari script, but I immediately fell in with the heart-rending cadence of these passionate stories of thwarted love, parental misdemeanours and dark family secrets. There was no confusion here between right and wrong – the heroines were torn only by contrition and remorse.

'I am an Indian woman,' I told myself, 'and for me my husband is my God.' So I got down to telephoning him. The old flat had no telephone, so I went to our neighbours and requested the use of their telephone to call Delhi. 'It's out of order,' they said sullenly. As the door clanged closed on my face, I heard the telephone ring, and a muttered conversation.

Resignedly, I walked over to the post office, and booked a call. The operator told me it would come through within half an hour. I began leafing through the telephone directory with pretended nonchalance. I did not want my tension and agony to become apparent to the indifferent P & T clerk. Idly, I began looking for the number of my old friend Mary – Mary Lobo now, she who had been resurrected with her letter about her lawyer brother. Evidently, she did not have a telephone at home. Her husband worked in a bank, so I looked up his office number. After I had located it I continued my frantic perusal of the directory. I even looked up B.R.'s number again. Just the sight of his name in cold print made me feel better. Finally my call came through. I was besides myself with nervous anticipation. Perspiration beaded my brow. '693211', the operator said, 'speak on to Delhi, dear.' A woman picked up the telephone. It was, unmistakably, Paro's voice. 'Hello,' she said, 'Hello, hello – damn – hello.' I was silent, then I mustered up the courage to say, 'Hello, may I speak to Suresh please?' But she had already put the phone down on the other end.

I didn't want the pain to show, at least not to the paan-chewing clerk. To cover my confusion, I dialled Mary's husband's number. I asked for Mr Lobo. 'Lobo here,' a voice answered.

'This is Priya, I'm an old friend of Mary's. We worked in office together. Could you ask her to give me a ring? No, I don't have a phone . . . my address is –' and to my horror I burst into tears. I sobbed out the address nevertheless. I paid the clerk, whose curiosity was still unaroused, and walked home through the dank puddly evening.

I didn't eat for two days after that. I just lay in bed, doing nothing, waiting for the doorbell to ring. I was sure that somebody or something would miraculously intervene to save me from this living death. I was engulfed by insecurity and terror. I wrote piteous letters to Suresh, dozens of them, begging his indulgence and pardon. I posted all of them.

I dreamt of Suresh during my troubled intermittent sleep, and in my dreams he was gallant, handsome and brave. I tried to send telepathic waves across the ether embracing him; I was demented by love and need. I looked up *Cheiro's Palmistry* and found it foretold a long and happy married life; I resisted the impulse to contact Dolly and Atul for emotional first aid.

Two days of near starvation made me feel euphoric. I went to the chemist and bought thirty Calmposes. I was sure that was enough to push me into death and oblivion. I swallowed them one by one, and contemplated leaving a suicide note. I decided my manuscript could speak for itself and did not need any addendum or apologia. I left it prominently beside my bedside and changed into a new chiffon sari. I sat before the spiteful old mirror and made myself up carefully. I wanted to look beautiful and triumphant in death. My eyelids were growing heavy and pendulous. Gratefully, I abandoned myself to sleep.

I awoke refreshed, still pleasantly euphoric, after what was only two hours by the dial of my wristwatch. I was not unduly disturbed by this failure of my death wish and decided to give it a last try. I left the house, saying a woozy goodbye to the photograph of my dead father which was the only photograph in the flat. Outside the building, on the way to the station, I bought a banana from the street vendor. I threw the skin into our neighbour's garden, and took the train into town, past all the old familiar stations.

I walked from Churchgate to Marine Drive. It was the evening rush-hour, and I felt peaceful in the embrace of the crowds. I sat on a bench for a long time, listening to the sad hungry conversation of the sea. It was ebb-tide. A narielpani-wala came over to where I was sitting and persuaded me to buy one. I sipped hungrily at the coconut water through the blue plastic straw he had provided. When I had finished, I tied the straw into a dozen knots and threw the coconut far into the sea. I weighed the different available methods of death by drowning. I could not swim, so I decided to walk into the water. I started off towards Nariman point; the monsoon breeze blew my sari up to my knees, like a ship in sail. I clambered down the rocks opposite the N.C.P.A. For a long time I stood looking at the bay; then, putting my purse down carefully by the shore, I waded in. The water was neither warm nor cold, it was viscous and friendly and it embraced me with a loving sensuality. I felt my cunt grow warm with the swirling currents. I think I was up to my waist in water. I wondered if anybody would notice me, but by then I was past caring, one way or the other.

Suddenly, I felt a sharp bite on my ankle, and a searing pain shot through my foot. Instinctively, I turned back towards the shore, writhing and screaming in agony. Even so, I did not forget to pick up my purse, and clutching it under my arm, I ran, demented by the growing pain, into Bombay. A jellyfish had intervened in this, my second brush with death.

I searched frantically for a taxi, for the pain had become unbearable by now. I couldn't find any through the furious traffic, so I hailed a Victoria. The driver eyed my soaked chiffon sari with curiosity, but he didn't say anything. 'Station,' I panted, 'Churchgate Station.' The clip-clop rhythm of the hooves, and the mad harmony of the pain hammered primordial songs in my wracked body. Suddenly, I spied the warm glow of lights from a familiar palm-fronted building. 'Stop,' I screamed. 'Roko, roko.' I handed him a fifty-rupee note and didn't wait for the change. I charged past the startled liftman and pressed the button for the second floor. The imitation-antique mahogany carved door was as immaculately polished as ever. I could hear the clear tone of the bell announcing my arrival. A bearer, still wearing an antiquated fan-turban, opened the door. 'B.R. Sahib,' I whispered, and pushed his startled figure aside and made for B.R.'s room.

He was lolling on a settee with his reading glasses on; a magazine dangled in his hands. 'Priya,' he said, a little taken aback by my unexpected and dishevelled visitation. 'What a delightful surprise! Why, is something the matter, love?'

'B.R.! Bubu!' The words fell like marbles from my crazed lips. 'I think a jellyfish has bitten me.' Immediately, he took control of the situation. He lay me down on the couch and rang the bell for the bearer.

'Ek whisky water and ek whisky neat ki darkhast hai,' he commanded. Miraculously, the drinks appeared. With sure deft hands, he began massaging my legs with the alcohol; the pain persisted, and I swooned, but not with pain alone. He handed me the other whisky to drink. Slowly, the pain subsided, or perhaps I just got used to it. Still he stroked my legs. His gentle fingers found their way upwards, and soon I found myself murmuring words of love. His lips sought mine, and the ecstasy of my love for him overtook me. Somewhere along the way I succumbed to the cumulative effect of the tranquillisers, the pain and the whisky; I awoke to find myself still in B.R.'s arms.

'I've given the bearer leave for the day,' he said. 'May I get you some breakfast?' But of course I protested, and made my way to the kitchen, and beat him a loving omelette. I was queen of the dark appliance-rich kitchen and revelled in the size and grandeur of his appetite. I nuzzled at his neck as he sipped at his coffee, and suddenly we were at lovemaking again. I was more awake and sentient this time. Stars and comets whizzed and sang about me. Finally, our passion exhausted, we fell to conversation.

'I've left them all,' I said light-heartedly. 'I've left Suresh and I've left Paro as well.'

He didn't look surprised even though that sounded a little strange. But a wary look crept into his eyes.

'Tell me,' he said, one eyebrow arched quizzically over his flashing eyes, 'how is my well-beloved ex-wife Paro? Still cashing in on the old magic?'

I was too happy and exhausted for that to hurt. 'She's OK, I suppose,' I replied.

'That lady, although she was my wife, is definitely one of the crudest, most castrating, selfish women I have ever encountered,' he continued. I nodded in understanding. A smile flickered in his eyes. 'You don't like her, do you?'

I considered the question for some time. I couldn't reply. 'I'm writing about her – a book,' I said finally.

He looked incredulous. 'You are writing a book?' The mantle of author fell like a benediction about me.

I told him all about it. He looked at me with a new respect. Indeed, he even looked a little wary. 'Am I in it?' he asked. I could see that his vanity was touched. 'Of course you are,' I replied.

'Is it a love story?' he asked teasingly.

'No,' I said.

'What is it about, then?'

I thought for a while. I thought of the dark sea, and the sharp, sure sting of the jellyfish, and of the sad stench of the ebb tide.

'Passion, boredom, vanity and jealousy,' I said finally, feeling a little pompous enunciating such long words.

'Come, love, tell me what it's really about,' he said.

'Liberation,' I hazarded.

That provoked him. 'Women's liberation?' he exclaimed. 'My author friend, can you in your book liberate me from the onerous responsibility of making love to every attractive or unattractive woman who uses me like a dildo to make her husband jealous? Can you liberate me from the financial burdens of alimony? Can you free me from the jealous possessiveness of the one woman I love? Can you bring up my children for me?' He was agitated, and a little out of breath.

He talked a lot, mostly about himself. Much of what

he said I had surmised anyway. But I had never really looked at the world through B.R.'s eyes, and for the first time I could recognise its troubled terrain and topography. He was quite feminine, really, in his meticulous love of detail; he had a frustrated homemaker hiding behind the lady-killer image. We skipped lunch, and at tea-time he got me some sandwiches. He took me out for dinner, and we chatted late into the night like old friends. There were even a few sets of spare clothing, frilly gowns and saris, which he said Bubbles had left behind. So I lay beside him, in my frilly nightgown, and crows cawed harshly outside, although it was the dead of night. They are disturbed by the light,' he said smiling mysteriously, and switched off the bedside lamp. We lay the night through in each other's arms.

I awoke before him the next morning. The bearer was back. He looked not at all surprised to find me there. 'Chai lao,' I said and settled down with the morning papers in the balcony.

The tea came on a silver teatray covered by a spotless white traycloth which had pretty, happy, pink roses embroidered over it. I poured it carefully from the silver teapot into the fine bone china teacup, and held the teacup daintily, with my little finger held artistically away. I sat thus, dreaming of harmony and beauty and perfect love; the morning noises from the pavement, the cry of the beggar child, the whine of the traffic, the whelp of street dogs, touched me not at all. After a while, B.R. appeared, smiling ever so gently, looking as soft and vulnerable as a small child. I poured him some tea, and handed him the morning papers.

'Priya, do you think I'm too old to get married again?' he asked me. It was a bolt from the blue.

'Are you asking me?' I said, startled and delighted.

Gentle reader, I married him. And we lived, as in a fairy tale, happily ever after.

'Of course I'm asking you,' he said. 'As my dearest, oldest, and most trusted friend, I want your advice. I'm in love for the first time – you know, truly in love. I love this ravishing girl who is as good as she is beautiful, only she's young enough to be my daughter! Her name's Maryann, Maryann Ruthers. She's an Aussie, of good ranching stock. She's studying economics in the States. Her father owns one of the largest cattle stations down under. And she loves me. For myself.'

I suppose it is a sign of my strength and resilience that my voice betrayed no tremor of either hope or dismay. Or perhaps I had never really dared to hope; I had only dreamt.

'Oh, congratulations,' I said brightly. 'That sounds wonderful. What does it feel like?' – remembering all the while a fairy story I had once read about a mermaid who loved a prince.

'Alas!' he sighed. 'For women there are always other men. But for men there are only other women. I suppose that sounds paradoxical, but, perhaps, I have finally come to terms with the impotence of my spirit.' He sighed again: 'Perhaps I'm getting old. Ah, youth, youth…'

'But you look as young as ever,' I breathed.

He ran his hands through his receding hair. 'I am, like Julius Caesar, a little vain about exposing my depleted cranium to the elements. It is,' he said pontifically, 'perhaps my only vanity.' With that, he rose majestically from his chair and disappeared to make his toilet. When he emerged, refreshed, redolent with cologne, I was still lost in my reveries.

'Well, Priya, my love, I must off to work,' he said heartily. 'I shall see you again when I return after a hard day's honest labour. Cook shall cater to you the luncheon of your choice. *Adieu*, or shall I say *au revoir*?'

'*Adieu*,' I said forlornly, and poured myself another cup of tepid tea. The bearer came in with a stack of magazines and laid them on the table. He took the teatray and left.

I curled up on the comfortable cane chair, sighed to the listening plants and picked up a magazine. The frizzy-haired, strident, somewhat raddled face on the cover looked familiar. It was, of course, Paro. CELEBRITY WEDDING OF THE YEAR the headline shrieked. Paro was dressed in a white wedding gown, with a veil and orange blossoms. On her arm she held a slight, lean man with hair down to his shoulders. He looked distinctly European. And very effete. I searched through the cover for any further clues. 'Loukas Leoros weds Indian Socialite,' it elaborated. That left me as much in the dark as before. Dazed, I rushed through the advertisements until I got to the lead story. It was a long and effusive article splashed with colour photographs. Suresh was conspicuous in many of them, looking surprisingly handsome in a dark suit. Next to him I could make out Bucky Bhandpur, looking busy and important and very flustered.

Paro was looking all in a haze, and quite pretty really. She was dressed in some photographs in traditional bridal clothes, and in others wore a white gown and Christian stuff. 'The bride, in vestal white and hymenal red, harmonising a happy blend of Orient and Occident,' the article gushed. 'A marriage of true minds,' it declared, and went on in hyperbolic prose about how 'a radiant, beautiful, utterly lovable and unconventional Indian beauty fell in love with and wed the *enfant terrible* of European Cinema, Loukas Leoros.

'Loukas Leoros,' the article continued, 'is a lonely stalker of reality. His cinema is stark and brooks no compromises. Familiar to film buffs the world over, he is today one of the foremost exponents of the cinema verité. He came to India to document on film the female anima, the compelling Lilith-like forces of Life, feminity, what we Hindu's call Maya. After a week's whirlwind romance, he has plunged headlong into his first matrimonial adventure. But his bride, Paro, is already a veteran of two marriages. Her ex-husband, Raja Birendra Singh of the erstwhile state of Bhandpur, was in fact the best man at the wedding. 'I knew when I met her,' Leoros says, 'that I had at last met my mother – for Paro is the universal mother!'

It all sounded like a lot of crap to me, from the ex post facto second marriage to all that Maya bit. But I was impressed; it was so like Paro to do something so totally mad and daring and unpredictable. The article gave discreet indication of Leoros's gay past, and of his recent passionate involvement with a young man. Memories stirred, and I remembered a snippet in *Time* magazine, in the 'People' page, about his acquittal in a lurid court case, and his open acknowledgement of his pederastic involvements.

I must say that I was impressed out of my wits. Trust Paro to hit yet another sixer. I felt quite self-congratulatory, and a bit of a celebrity myself, actually knowing someone who was married to someone who featured in *Time* magazine!

'Our correspondent in Delhi sought an interview with the newly-weds,' the magazine continued. 'The new Mrs Loukas was ensconced in her fabulous hotel suite, surrounded by trillions of flowers, and with her young son Aniruddha, down from university hostel for the wedding, beside her. She categorically refused to answer any personal questions, insisting that "We live in a world of stereotypes. But Loukas is a prototype. I have nothing further to say!" '

I bet she read that somewhere, she couldn't have thought it up on the spur of the moment.

'As a wedding gift, Leoros is rumoured to have presented to his wife a priceless antique sword belonging to one of the Royal families. He is even said to have had her name specially inscribed upon the hilt with rubies and diamonds.' I read and re-read the article several times. I absorbed it, and learnt it by rote, and tried to extract as much detail and information as I possibly could out of the unresponsive printed page.

I wondered what B.R. would have to say. It was quite possible that he had known already. It would surely be irritating to his vanity to have Paro in the arms of yet another lover. Only a confessed homosexual, I reflected wryly, could have the determination and stamina to take on Paro. Her need to live was so total, greedy and heedless, that she would doubtless have exhausted anyone in the sexual fray.

I sat around for a long time after that. The bearer asked me what I would like for lunch. I wasn't hungry, I replied. He didn't insist.

I wandered into B.R.'s study. The walls were lined with solid-looking shelves crammed with books. On his desk stood a photograph of his father, the Rai Bahadur, dead these five years, but malevolent still through the gilt frame. A familiar terror stirred in me and I moved towards the bookshelves. Well-thumbed leatherbound volumes on Art, Poetry and History confronted me. I extracted one and began leafing through it. Naked young girls with airbrushed pubic hair cavorted from the faded sheets. I looked to the discreet maroon binding. 'Playboy, April – Sept. 3.' it read in gold letters down the spine. I looked around me and discovered that B.R. had, with a collector's passion, preserved every single issue of Playboy, circa 1960 onwards!

I sort of mulled things over for a while. Then, resolutely, I walked to the telephone and dialled Delhi. Magically, I got through the very first time. An unfamiliar voice answered. 'Is sahib there?' I asked.

'Sahib is still in court,' came the reply. I put the receiver down and waited precisely until four. Then I telephoned again. Suresh picked it up this time. 'This is Priya speaking, Suresh,' I said tonelessly, the hope and terror concealed somewhere in my larynx. 'Can I return home please?'

'I received your letters,' he replied. 'If that is how you feel, perhaps we can give it a try again.'

'I'll be there tomorrow,' I said, and tried to contain the sudden surge of joy. My knees were weak with relief.

I left a note for B.R. and gave it to the bearer. I walked all the way to Churchgate Station, and from there took a local to Bombay Central. Of course they could not give me a reservation for Delhi. But a sleazy footpathwala with the right connections helped me out. I bought a third-class ticket and got it converted on payment of a small bribe. I felt reassured by the crowds, the press of humanity, the noise and the dirt. I settled down by a window seat. Faces swam before me on the platform. Then, the long sharp whistle, and the train left. Past Dadar, past Mahim, past Andheri, to Delhi. I thought, in a tired sort of way, of my life. I thought of B.R. and Suresh, and Lenin. And I saluted Paro's courage.

Two women sitting opposite were discussing Amitabh Bachhan. 'Jayaji is really aaj-ki-Sita,' one said smugly. The other woman took objection to that. 'Hah, she should have left Amitabh long ago. Now, that Rekha, she is what I call a woman. The trouble with these Indian men is that they're all after one thing only.'

I returned home. Life soon resumed a timorous momentum. We had a new domestic servant, for Ratan Singh had gone home to his village for something or the other. Suresh had had the house painted, and everything seemed efficient and well managed. Suresh took great pains to be nice to me, although I could sense some withdrawal behind his hardworking, cosmetic concern.

We seldom discussed Paro, or the past, with each other. There was a void in our lives without her, but it also assumed a certain pleasant predictability. She sent Suresh a case of Chianti for his birthday through an Embassy friend.

It took us almost a year to consume it, for it was brought out only for Very Special Friends or Clients and every glass prefaced with a short speech about the sender, her international jet-set lifestyle, and what a dear close friend she was, really. After each bottle was consumed, I ritually planted a moneyplant in it, and by the time a year was out our bedroom, all the bathrooms and the balcony were full of moneyplants creeping energetically out of straw-covered Chianti bottles. They all prospered.

We seriously considered adopting a child. Our friends all advised us against it, but Suresh was quite keen on the idea. He wanted a son. I was indifferent but I could picture myself grooming a pretty little girl into womanhood. We even went to an orphanage and inspected several children in a damp silent office. They entered solemnly, one by one, and sat by turns on a wooden chair before us, framed in the distance by a life-size portrait of grinning, toothless, gleeful Gandhiji. Two of the boys seemed very clever and bright, and though they didn't speak English, appeared well versed in Geography, Algebra, and the general knowledge questions with which Suresh gravely interrogated them.

But we heard them shuffling and shouting 'Bhenchut' to each other in the corridor outside after they left, and I knew their fate was sealed, at least as far as getting Suresh for a parent was concerned.

The third child was a thin, fair, fragile and very pretty girl. She balanced each of her birdlike arms upon the stiff wooden armrests, and the plastic bangles she was wearing made even that dour office look festive. She too seemed to know the answers to all the random pointless questions that Suresh directed at her, and I wondered whether they had been coached and tutored in the appropriate responses. Then she left, flashing a shy delightful smile, as she shut the door behind her, and my heart was molten with love and longing to have her for my daughter.

But of course we didn't adopt a child. We settled for a pet instead. I wanted an apso but Suresh bought a snappy little pomeranian from a junior in his office, a girl whose brother bred dogs. We named her Lady; she barked incessantly and disliked me intensely. The feeling was reciprocated, and I dreamt often of quietly mixing an obscure poison into her milk and eggs and crumbled bread.

*

Except that the sofas were covered with white dog

143

hair, life continued much as usual. Then, a few days before Diwali, when the air was already acrid with the sounds and smells of fireworks, Paro returned. Her reappearance into my life was, as ever, heralded by dramatic coincidence. It was a Saturday evening, and Doordarshan was broadcasting Devdas. I had always wanted to see the film, for I knew a Paro too, and I had just settled down before the television, alone, for Suresh had gone to Madras for a case. The telephone rang with the special shrill insistence of her calls. 'Hi, darling, how are you? Still the same darling old Priya?' she asked breezily. 'Watching me on TV? And what's lawyer sahib doing so far away in Madras?'

How did she always know everything, I wondered miserably, how did she manage to do it? 'When did you come in, Paro?' I asked brightly.

'Half an hour ago, love, and I'm trying to get the gang together for auld lang syne.' There was no contempt in her voice. For a change, she sounded almost friendly.

Half an hour found me outside her suite in the Taj. Raucous sounds filtered through the half-open door. There they were, all her ragged Caravanserai... Bucky Bhandpur, grinning in his toothy affectionate way, and as urbane and self-assured as ever; Junior, even more heartbreakingly handsome in his first bristly glow of adolescent youth; all the arty crowd of her theatre days; and Lenin – yes, Lenin, with his strong determined wife in an advanced stage of pregnancy, seated by his side, a glass balanced upon her belly. There were also some of Paro's firangi friends from the Embassy, and a morose-looking Iranian she had picked up on the plane, who she mockingly introduced around as the Ayatollah. Paro herself lolled regally on the sofa; she had become massively fat, and was dressed in something I can't even begin to describe. She wore her corpulence like expensive jewellery, and her eyes glittered like sapphires.

The doorbell rang, and again I could hear a prescient foreboding in its innocuous trill. Lenin opened the door, and we found B.R. and his young new Australian wife framed in the euphoric cigarette haze, standing as though for a portrait.

'Bubu,' Paro screamed, and sheathed him in a joyous embrace. I couldn't even see if he was resisting, for she wrapped him as completely as a banana skin. He emerged, smothered but smiling, and planted a decorous kiss on her excited cheek. Both of them ignored his wife completely.

'So, wife of my youth, what brings you to these distant waters?' B.R. intoned melodiously.

'I feel like a cat on a hot tin roof; I'm in heat; I need a man! And Loukas, as we all know, is a woman. But he's a dreadfully jealous woman. And of course I wanted to see Junior in the holidays,' she said deadpan. I was inured to her thoughtless blasphemous blabber, but nevertheless looked around, a little shocked, for the others' reactions. The Australian girl-child looked a little bewildered, and Lenin's wife seemed about to stage a walk-out, which indeed she shortly did.

Paro's son smiled, a little tremulously, I thought. But he seemed to take it in his stride. An indulgent child.

145

'Really, Paro,' Lenin remonstrated gently.

'Why, can't a woman feel horny?' she retorted. It was at this stage that Lenin's wife got up and awkwardly waddled her way out, her arms held around her belly as if to protect her unborn child from such conversation.

'Lenin, please say goodbye to your friends or I will miss the train,' she said, her jaw protruding at an alarmingly angry angle.

'She has to go to Jabbalpur with her sister; we want to have the delivery at home,' Lenin explained appeasingly. And so the two of them left.

B.R. in the meanwhile, was breathing heavily at Paro, and Paro, too, was emitting peculiar auditory signals. She was quite sozzled, being already on her nth Campari, and stomped her predatory way, thomp thomp thomp, barefoot, scarlet-toenailed, towards B.R. and settled herself upon his lap. He winced in pain, and adjusted her weight within the confines of the elegant gilt chair. It was obvious that the old chemistry was at work between them. B.R. had not even noticed my presence.

Everybody went on drinking, and talking, and munching at cashew nuts, which were soon strewn like confetti over the carpet. Junior had, with the urbanity and breeding he had doubtless inherited from Bucky, decided to compensate for his mother's impoliteness by concentrating upon Maryann, who was, as far as I could gather, shooting off penetrating questions about inflation which he was gamely parrying. They looked very right and complete together, and I felt like a fairy godmother, and wished I had a wand to bind their incongruous youthful unity. Bucky was tapping his pipe and smiling benevolently into space, and the arty theatre crowd were all, I suspected, spaced out on hash and alcohol, and seemed quite at peace with themselves and the world. They were gently but forcefully debating the relative merits of film and theatre.

'Drama happens,' I heard Krishen declaim, 'and interacts with the viewer, whilst film is essentially a fascist medium, imposing preconceived images on the viewer which are ultimately incapable of ambiguous interpretation.'

While I was trying to figure that one out, I spied Paro nuzzling delicately at B.R.'s cheeks and modestly averted my gaze. When I had recovered enough to look in that direction again, they had left for the adjoining bedroom, the door of which they had left discreetly ajar.

Maryann was feeling quite distressed by now, and Junior asked if she would like to go to the disco downstairs for a while. She flicked back her straight blonde hair, smiled thankfully, and they too departed, leaving only the theatre vs. film agitators, with Bucky as a benevolent but indifferent presiding jurist. And of course me, voyeur and diarist. Even the morose Iranian had fled.

Bucky was just enquiring gravely about Suresh, and whether Lady, our bitch, had her rabies shots regularly, and other such polite queries about my family life, when Lenin walked in, divested of his sentry wife, looking Christ-like and young again. 'Where is she?' he asked, his eyes sifting through the theatre crowd, who were by now beginning to get a little acrimonious. No one even bothered to reply. So he stalked into the next room. What happened then is history.

'I saw his hairy thighs around her. He was fucking her…' Lenin said, tears streaming from his eyes. 'What are you doing, Paro?' I screamed. She sat up, all mussed up and dishevelled, she hadn't taken off her clothes. He was in his shirt, and he hadn't even taken off his trousers!' Somehow this fact seemed to agitate him most.

'Well, all of us just sat down, and he pulled up his pants, and Paro phoned room service to get me a drink. We just sort of looked at each other, and then B.R. went off in search of Maryann. I felt so betrayed, it was like witnessing a Primal Scene.'

I didn't know what a Primal Scene was, and he explained that it was the trauma of witnessing your father and mother copulating. I told him that every Indian child living in a chawl watched it every day and didn't get so worked up, and break down and things, but I couldn't hold his attention, and he continued with his own train of thought.

'Geeta had left for Jabbalpur, and Maryann and Junior were downstairs at the Disco. I was sobbing with rage and jealousy, and Paro gave me a tight slap, I mean she literally left a five-finger imprint on my cheek. I gave her my other cheek, and she slapped that too. "After all, he was my fucking husband," she said, and then she kissed me, and called me her baby, and we went in search of them. They were sitting downstairs, having a soft drink, and this guy B.R. was having a jealous fit that Maryann should be with Junior. Christ!

'I said that I was leaving, but Paro wouldn't let me. She was getting very agitated – I think she was feeling jealous of Maryann. [On account of B.R. or Junior, I wondered.] So Junior said he was going upstairs. He had a room adjoining hers, you know. "Why don't you take Ma for a drive and calm her down," he said.

'So we went off for a drive, and, man, was she pissed. I suppose I was too. We got into the car, and we started driving round and round, and she started crying, saying that I had let her down by getting married. The more I tried to comfort her the more worked up she got. She said it was because of my infidelity, imagine, my infidelity, that she had married this Loukas character, even though she knew he was a homosexual. And she said he put her on a pedestal but she had feet of clay, and she wanted sex, and she hadn't had any sex since she got married. I said everybody in Greece couldn't be homosexual, but she said he put private detectives on her who trailed her all the time as he had a Madonna complex and wanted her inviolate. I thought that was really funny, and looked behind to see if anyone was following us. So the car sort of swerved, and we hit the kerb, and there we were in front of a flower shop. You know, that all-night kiosk in Janpath. She began kissing me, and slobbering all over me, no disrespect meant, and soon we were kissing each other passionately, and to be truthful it really excited me, to think that I had just seen her fucking him; it disgusted me but it excited me as well, I was in love with her and I hated her, I felt as though I was being throttled by a

149

panther or something.

'So I got out of the car and walked over to the flower shop. I bought up the shop, I mean all the goddamn flowers they had in stock. So they started shoving all those bucketfuls of flowers into the car, and Paro was absolutely delighted. It was just the kind of dramatic gesture that appealed to her. So I paid the guy, and we drove off again. She insisted on driving, and she seemed quite steady on the wheel at first. The car was smelling like a hearse, stuffed with mogra and tuberoses and narcissus, and her perfume and the stink of liquor – I was pissed myself, but even I could smell it. I remember seeing some rockets flashing across the sky, it was around Diwali time, remember, and then there was this fruit truck ahead, and then a massive crash and then I passed out.

'When I came to I found a large crowd around us, and Paro was covered with blood, and squashed fruits, and vegetables, and all those flowers. I remember there was a sitaphal, you know, a custard apple, splashed all over the windscreen.

'I was right as rain, but she looked as if it were all over. The crowd thought she was dead, too, and they were quite excited. An ambulance came and took us to the hospital. I was a little zonked, but she had been driving, and the steering had mashed her up. There was a police van as well, and even though I thought she was dead all I could worry about was what Geeta would say. I was petrified, she is a very strong woman, you know.

'So I left her at the A.I.I.M.S. and went off to the phone booth. Everyone at the casualty ward was moaning and groaning like something out of Dante's *Inferno*. I was convinced that she was dead. So I left her to the doctors and brushed off the policemen and rushed to telephone Mishraji. He was the only man who could get me out of that hell. So he phoned the Home Minister, and somebody telephoned somebody, and the police were quite nice, and said they would interrogate me later. And we got the newspapers to sort of play it down, and it turned out from Police investigations that it was all the fruit-truckwallah's fault anyway. He had overloaded his truck with all those fucking fruits and vegetables; I think he got a fracture or something.

'Geeta returned the next day. She was very nice about it, very righteous and understanding. She insisted that we visit Paro at the hospital. By then Leoros had returned as well, with a pansy secretary to hold his hand, and he was really hysterical about the whole thing. Luckily he didn't know all the details. Paro was asleep when we visited her at the hospy, she looked weird. She had broken her jaw and they hadn't quite set it. She lost half her teeth, you know.'

I remembered her, propped up in the hospital bed. She was having quite a grand time, really. Death seemed to have just grazed her. It was nowhere lurking in that festive hospital room, overflowing as it was with cards and flowers and celebrity visitors.

Maryann had been furious, and hurt, and upset, and B.R. was entirely caught up in placating her. They sent her a basket of fruit and flowers, which Paro had removed from the room. 'Considering the circumstances of my accident, a tactless gift,' she had said coldly.

'Now I can really give it to Luke, Priya,' she had murmured through that shattered face. 'Without those goddamn teeth I'll blow the bugger out of his mind.' She grinned gleefully, like a satyr, then winced with pain at the effort, and the doctor had to be called in.

I brushed the memories aside, for Lenin was much too involved in his own version of things. 'I'm to blame,' he insisted, 'it was I who killed her.' Perhaps he was feeling left out by the circumstances of her death. We were still circling the deserted Delhi streets. They were lit as though for a party; the Asian Games were due to begin the next day. 'It's all my fault,' he said again.

But I was only half listening. Paro was dead. I had watched her die. Lenin had nothing to do with it at all.

She had a party to celebrate her recovery. I was getting a little tired of parties, and, to my amazement, it appeared as though Paro was too. She had sort of shrivelled up after the accident, like an apple that has been stored too long; she seemed tense and withdrawn and somehow diminished. She sipped morosely at her whisky and watched Suresh and Bucky and me watching our Paro and trying to celebrate her return to health. A funny film unfolded on the TV in the corner, unwatched. Leoros's secretary, Tony, was there as well; he was attending on Loukas, who was attending on Paro. One foot was still in plaster, and she was hobbling indelicately. She had changed her hairstyle, had it cut to her shoulders; and, to my intense surprise, it wasn't frizzy any more.

Leoros was hovering behind her like an anxious waiter, as though he didn't dare look her in the eyes. His limbs described limp, floppy arcs as he droned on and on about his diminishing creativity. 'My gift . . . it is failing!' he wailed.

Paro looked at him venomously. He didn't notice.

'The vision,' he continued, pointing each of his fingers towards his eyes in explicit explanation, 'the vision. . . it is blurring.' Bhandpur listened impassively; he was digging into a large glittering box of chocolates while Suresh was masticating his way through a bowl of salted cashew nuts.

Just then, I noticed Tony staring at Paro, hatred incandescent in his young face. It was a beautiful face – a sullen, sulky, pouting boy's face, with the pinkest, fullest lips I had ever seen.

'But the force,' Leoros continued, 'the creative force… it can redeem… it can be… how you say… renewed.' And he scurried to the bedroom, and emerged with a jewelled sword. It was the pair of the one he had given Paro at their wedding.

'I bought this as a present for Paro,' he said, flourishing it at us. Bhandpur examined it knowledgeably. Tony ran his long, slim fingers over its cool surface.

Paro stared at them savagely. 'Bloody fruits,' she murmured.

Tony reacted furiously. 'What did you say?' he hissed, in his peculiar accent.

'Bloody fruits,' she said loudly enough for a lip-reader to hear.

'Say that again,' Tony said through clenched teeth, his voice assuming an almost masculine timbre.

'Why, didn't you hear?' she enquired, an infuriating smile playing on her lips.

She seemed to be waking up, somehow. I could almost see the soft down on her white arms gently waving, like in a biology film. She was blooming again. Her wrinkled white skin smoothed out, her eyes flashed. She gorged herself on the angry excitement. Leoros wrung his hands despairingly. 'Don't get agitated, angel,' she said coldly, her eyes narrowed.

'Don't call me that,' Tony said, his eyes liquid with anger.

Suresh was still munching at cashew nuts, a glazed look in his eyes. A furtive excitement gripped me. Loukas looked appeasingly at all of us. Tony took the sword and unsheathed it again. Tears gleamed in his eyes; his long, black eyelashes could scarcely contain them. Paro got up and hobbled to the bathroom.

Tony was still staring at the sword when she returned. Leoros was staring beseechingly at Tony. 'Now, darlings, don't let's get phallic,' she said, the infuriating smile still dancing on her lips. They didn't respond. They just continued to stare into each other's eyes. The television film came to an abrupt end; the blank screen flashed funny lights and signals and geometric designs. A waiter came in from Room Service with some ice. Bhandpur signed the bill. Still they stared.

Suddenly Paro lunged towards the fruit basket on the table by her side. She took the knife and hurled it at the window. It fell on the sofa opposite. Nobody responded, she took the ashtray and threw it in the same direction. It landed silently on the carpet; it didn't break.

Leoros and Tony were staring at her in astonishment. Suresh seemed oblivious to the tension, and I had witnessed such scenes too many times before. Bhandpur poured her a drink. Tony flounced out of the room, banging the door behind him. Leoros switched off the television.

It was all like a jerky film, running at different speeds, out of synch. Suddenly, everyone was animated again. Everyone, that is, except Paro. She lifted herself heavily from the sofa and dragged herself to the window. I can see her, staring moodily out of the panes, which had misted up in the winter cold. It was raining softly outside, and the cars on the street were wet blurry streaks of light. I think I saw tears in her eyes. Her hair tumbled over her face. She sat hunched up, stony-faced, yet somehow more defenceless than I had ever seen her.

Nobody was having fun. I saw Paro staring, fascinated, at her wrists. They were dripping blood. She had slashed them with the fruit knife.

'Paro,' I screamed, and rushed to her side. I splashed the watery ice on her wrists, and searched frantically for something to bandage her with. I could find nothing. I tore a strip off my sari pallav. The blood was spurting out. It didn't seem to stop.

'Come with me to the hospital, Suresh,' Bhandpur said uncertainly. 'Priya, you telephone and tell them we are coming.' He ignored Leoros altogether, and before I knew it they had left.

I waited in the empty room. There were empty glasses and choked ashtrays all around. Leoros disappeared as well. After a long time the phone rang. Paro was dead.

Paro was dead. I couldn't imagine a world without her. I sat and thought for a long time, but no thoughts came. I got up, and emptied the ashtrays, and remembered Paro in the hospital, many years ago, with bandaged wrists, but she had survived. There were dark stains on the carpet, and my sari pallav was torn. She couldn't breathe, she couldn't move, she couldn't be mean to me any more. I looked at the empty chair. She hadn't meant to die; I was sure about that. It was just a silly accident, a tantrum. But then, she had looked so despairing, staring out of the window, her hair falling about her face – and now she was dead.

I didn't go to the funeral. Loukas was too ill to decide anything. He was red-eyed, as though from too much drinking, Loukas who dissected death and tragedy in his films every day. His psychiatrist had flown in from Europe. Bucky Bhandpur took over; their son would light the pyre. No electric cremation, he insisted grimly, but the proper Hindu rites. Suresh went to the cremation grounds, and wouldn't say a word after he returned. He simply took a lot of tranquillisers, and locked himself into our bedroom, requesting me to please sleep in the guest room and not disturb him until the next morning.

So I had my dinner, and was sitting over the

newspapers, which were full of the tragedy, when Lenin came in, looking completely shattered. 'Geeta has had a miscarriage,' he said, 'and it was a boy.' He made it sound as though that made it a little more tragic.

And then he started talking obsessively about how it hadn't been his fault, how none of it had been his fault at all. I stroked his damp forehead and told him it was all right, it wasn't his fault at all. I poured him a whisky although it was clear he had already had too much to drink.

'I've run out of fags,' he said, 'do you have any?' But Suresh had stopped smoking long ago and we got them only for parties.

'Come with me to the paan shop,' he said, 'I can't bear to be alone tonight.' So we drove off in his Fiat. He bought the cigarettes, but we didn't return home. He had to strike the match several times, his hands were shaking so. 'Let's drive around for a while,' he said, 'just like we did that day.' And so we circled those silent streets. He switched on some muzak with trembling fingers and continued to talk compulsively.

We were on the ring road now, near Rajghat and Shantivana. There was a man slouching indolently astride a donkey ahead of us. Disco music blared from the car stereo. Tears streamed down Lenin's eyes. Suddenly we had collided with the donkey, and the man tumbled off. The donkey whinnied in pain. The man came towards us. 'Abbe, ghat pahunchayega,' he said abusively. Lenin extracted a hundred-rupee note from his pocket and held it towards him. He loped off, still mouthing obscenities.

That triggered something in Lenin's mind. 'Let's go,' he said urgently, 'let's go to the ghat. Paro's alone there.' I began feeling a little creepy.

We drove past the shanties and parked carts, our arrival heralded by the music blaring from the stereo.

'Paro's dead, Lenin,' I remonstrated, 'and we have to forget the past and leave the dead in peace.' A certain relief, even triumph, in the act of survival, in outwitting Paro, filtered through. 'Geeta will be waiting for you,' I chided.

'Don't talk about them in the same breath,' he said savagely. I fell silent. I knew reasoning would not work with Lenin in his present frame of mind. All I could do was fumble with the stereo, but I couldn't find the switch.

We entered through somewhat ornate gates. There were bodies burning in neat little rows right from the entrance. No one seemed to be around. Some of the fires were burning high and bright; others were almost extinguished. What struck me most was the ugliness of the architecture – its coy ornate pretentiousness in the face of what was, after all, death. We sat down together on a bench. Lenin was still weeping copiously. It was not cold, even though the Yamuna flowed just beyond. I suppose it was because of the bodies. 'Can you hear the river?' Lenin asked in sudden ecstasy. I confessed I could not. 'See… can't you hear the murmur,' he asked. I prodded him gently and begged him to get up. The place was peaceful enough, but I was uneasy. 'All right, if you insist,' he said indifferently, and we shuffled silently through those rows of smouldering pyres. Suddenly, we were surrounded by the sadistic officialdom of the burning ghats. Four men, cloaked in coarse woollen blankets, encircled us. Each held a hefty bamboo in his hand. The fires illuminated their gloomy, suspicious faces. 'What you are doing here?' they asked.

'Nothing,' I replied. 'A friend of ours had died and this gentleman wanted to come and pay his last respects.'

'What he was to you?' one of them asked next.

'Nothing,' I confessed.

'Wait,' he said, and the four of them huddled into a conclave like so many indecisive yamadoots.

They reappeared a few minutes later. 'This is very wrong,' they said, 'Bhai Sahib, we will have to do an enquiry. You have a Ladies with you, and your mouth is smelling of the whisky. Disco music is blowing from your car. You have come for the wrong act.'

I was outraged. He thought we had come to copulate! But Lenin slipped his hand into his pocket and drew out another hundred-rupee note.

They grabbed it officiously, and left, murmuring something about duty being, after all, duty.

And so we left. The pyre ahead of us, the first one, burnt even more furiously; the glorious orange glow seemed strong and comforting. A stray ember rose and floated in the cold night air like a benediction; then fell on my sari pallav.

As we left, I wondered what they had done with Lenin's baby. The hospital had disposed of mine.

Lenin dropped me home. I fell into exhausted, dreamless sleep. The next morning, Suresh and I met at the breakfast table. I told him nothing about the previous evening. Our maid, who did the washing, came up to me self-righteously. 'Memsahib, your sari is burnt already, I did nothing,' she said accusingly.

'It's all right,' I said dismissively, and she left.

'Suresh, where exactly was Paro's body burnt?' I asked.

'In the raised pyre, the V.I.P. one,' he replied matter-of-factly.

I got up from the table, feeling suddenly very ill. I threw up my breakfast. And with that benediction from the stranger's pyre, I end this book.

ABOUT THE AUTHOR

Namita Gokhale is a writer and co-founder and co-director of the famed Jaipur Literature Festival. She is the author of twenty-five books, including fourteen works of fiction. Her novels include *Never Never Land*, *The Blind Matriarch* and *Jaipur Journals*. Her non-fiction includes *Mystics and Sceptics: In Search of Himalayan Masters* and the anthology *Treasures of Lakshmi*.

Gokhale has been recognized both for her writing and her commitment to multilingual Indian literature and cross-cultural literary dialogue. She has received numerous awards including the First Centenary National Award for Literature in 2017 and the prestigious Sahitya Akademi (National Academy of Literature) Award 2021 for her novel *Things to Leave Behind*. She has been honoured with the Nilimarani Sahitya Samman 2023.

ABOUT THE AUTHOR OF THE INTRODUCTION

Maya Jaggie was elected a fellow of the Royal Society of Literature in 2023 for her award-winning, independent critical writing on global art and books. She is a contributing art critic to the *Financial Times* and was a cultural writer and a lead fiction critic for the *Guardian* for a decade, writing profiles of a dozen Nobel laureates in literature and figures from Umberto Eco to Arundhati Roy. She was a finalist for the Orwell Prize for Journalism, and her writing has appeared widely, including in the *New York Review of Books*, *The New York Times*, *The Economist* and *Le Monde Diplomatique*. She has been an Associate Fellow of Warwick University, a DAAD Arts and Media Fellow in Berlin, an EU Senior Expert in cultural journalism in post-Soviet capitals, and chair of judges of the European Bank for Reconstruction and Development (EBRD) Literature Prize 2024-5. She has an honorary doctorate from the Open University for 'extending the map of international writing,' and degrees from Oxford University and LSE.

ABOUT HOPEROAD PUBLISHING

HopeRoad was founded in 2010 by Rosemarie Hudson, a publisher who's spent her life encouraging exciting new talent, mentoring and publishing new authors and bringing them to wider attention. Often hailed as a 'trailblazer', she's always promoted the best writing from and about Africa, Asia and the Caribbean. And it's thanks to her HopeRoad is known as the indie which loves to share untold stories around themes of identity, cultural stereotyping, disability and injustice.

Rosemarie was joined in her venture by Pete Ayrton, founder of the hugely respected independent publisher Serpent's Tail. Pete heads up HopeRoad's imprint, Small Axes, which republishes out of print post-colonial classics – books which shaped cultural shifts at the time they were first in print, and remain as relevant today.

HopeRoad recently joined forces with Peepal Tree Press. Working together they will make a significant contribution to the diversity of independent publishing in the UK, giving voice to the underrepresented. Both share a long-term commitment to literary values that is not dictated by fashion, as well as a compatible ethos, backlists and complementary publishing identities.

By reading, buying or borrowing this book you're helping to support authors at a time when their ideas are needed more than ever.

Keep up to date with what's new through our newsletter at https://www.hoperoadpublishing.com/about, discover all HopeRoad and Small Axes titles at https://www.hoperoadpublishing.com/, and join the debate on social media at @hoperoadpublishing and @hoperoadpublish.